BREAK IN
COMMUNICATION

BREAK IN COMMUNICATION

RAID ON PORTHCURNO TELEGRAPH STATION, CORNWALL DURING WWII

JON GLIDDON

THE CHOIR PRESS

First published in the United Kingdom in 2015 by
The Choir Press

ISBN 978-1-910864-06-7

Contents

Monday 15 December 1941 – 4.00 pm

Bristol, South West England

In the shadows of the station concourse a tall, lean figure surveyed his would-be fellow travellers with distrust. His heavy black trench coat with collar up protected him from the biting east wind swirling down the exposed platform. The black Fedora hat pulled down over his steel-grey eyes helped to keep the cold at bay but more importantly afforded some anonymity. A brown leather, weather-beaten suitcase was tightly gripped in his gloved left hand, and his right hand was thrust deep in his coat pocket.

A tannoy boomed, 'The next train arriving at platform six is the 4.15 to Penzance calling at Exeter St David's, Newton Abbot, Plymouth ...' and on it droned through the long list of stations, but the Stranger wasn't listening. He was looking around intently, his eyes flicking left and right under the brow of his hat. He scrutinised the huddle of waiting passengers but saw nothing immediately suspicious. In the background, a paperboy was shouting, 'Evenin' Post get yur Evenin' Post, latest on the bommins'. The Stranger walked to the news stand, bought a paper, glanced back but saw no one following and moved on down the platform towards the huddle of passengers. He stood by a pillar and raised the paper as if reading, but he wasn't; he was uneasy, his heart was racing. He knew intuitively there was going to be trouble; he just knew it.

He was on the last leg of his long journey and he was tired, needed to sleep, and a meal wouldn't go amiss. He hadn't eaten a decent meal since ... when? He couldn't remember. But thus far he'd had free passage with identity papers checked by inattentive policemen who wouldn't know a forged document if it jumped up and bit them. But since the meeting with his English contact two days ago he'd been on heightened alert. In his mind, he questioned the decision to take a mainline train, but he now had no option; he was on a tight schedule. He folded the newspaper under his arm and slipped his right hand into his coat pocket and caressed the handle of his cold, steel, stiletto knife.

The announced train hissed and clanked along the platform and screeched to a halt in a swirl of steam. The smell of coal smoke and hot oil filled his nostrils. For a split second it took him straight back to his childhood in The Cape and his father taking him for rides on the footplate of his Garratt locomotive. 'Temple Meads, this is Bristol Temple Meads,' boomed the tannoy, shaking him from his momentary reverie.

A large number of people were waiting to get on. Train services were hit-and-miss with the disruptive bombing, and when there was a train, passengers were intent on getting a seat. Polite British queuing had been abandoned for the war. In the crush the Stranger barged his way onto a carriage and searched out a compartment with a space. He had a long journey ahead of him and didn't want to stand all the way. In the fifth one he found a vacant seat by the window; not an ideal location but it would do. He squeezed through, put his brown leather suitcase in the overhead rack and sat down. It was roasting hot by comparison with the platform, and the smell of sour sweat hit his nostrils. Jesus, don't these people wash? he thought.

After what seemed an eternity to him, the train whistled and jolted forward. Slowly and noisily, it pulled out of the station on its journey west. He was still concerned about being followed and eased the blackout blind a fraction to check the platform. To his dismay, he saw two policemen running down the platform followed by a man in a brown tweed coat. They ran toward the back of the train and he lost them from view. He couldn't see if they'd got on; he had to assume they had; he was glad he had checked.

The old woman opposite tut-tutted and said, 'Mind that blind, young man, there is a blackout, you know.'

The Stranger glowered at her. Bossy old cow, he thought, who the hell does she think she's talking to?

He eyed the other passengers: the bossy old cow sat opposite and next to her another old lady, probably a companion. A couple with a young child sat on his side of the compartment by the door, and a middle aged man and woman sat opposite them. He studied the couple; he was reading a newspaper, but seemed innocent enough. His wife was very shapely indeed, nice ankles, he thought but quickly steered his mind back to his immediate predicament; had the police got on the train?

The young girl beside him constantly whined to the annoyance of everyone in the compartment, except her parents. The Stranger was anxious and felt tempted to clip her around the ear but he thought, relax man, relax, that won't help you and besides she and her mother might well come in handy if things get serious. His steely eyes watched the door as he worked through his options. It was still hot in the carriage and he removed his Fedora to uncover a gaunt, tanned face with black, brushed-back hair, touched with grey around the ears. But he didn't remove his coat; he kept his right hand thrust in the pocket.

'Do you mind?' said the old cow's companion, shaking the Stranger from his thoughts. 'Could I look at your newspaper, if you've finished with it?'

The Stranger handed it to her with a smile on his lips but not in his eyes. The young family next to him drank tea from a flask and shared some sandwiches, although the girl complained they were stale and that her mother should know she doesn't eat spam. Little brat, he thought. Christ, he was hungry; his stomach rumbled.

The door slid open and a uniformed man appeared. The Stranger's heart leapt and his right hand tensed; he had been miles away in the heat of the carriage and preoccupation with his companions.

'Tickets please, ladies and gentlemen,' said the train guard, 'tickets please.' The Stranger breathed deeply and passed his ticket with a smile, but even so, he felt the guard held his gaze a little longer than necessary. Nervous, when the guard left he debated whether to move or stay where he was. He chose to stay.

His level of anxiety rose in anticipation of an impending visit, but thirty minutes later he had started to relax again; perhaps they hadn't got on, he thought. He started to rehearse in his mind the task he'd been assigned.

'Difficult, dangerous and urgent,' his contact had said. He worked through the briefing he'd been given and the further contact he had to make.

3

After nearly an hour the train came to a sudden lurching stop, wheels screeching, and immediately the carriage lights went out. There were exclamations from the passengers and a palpable unease.

'Oh goodness, has there been an accident, do you think?' asked the old cow's companion.

'No, I don't think so,' said the young father, 'we're probably letting a priority train pass.'

The Stranger was taking no chances; he gripped the stiletto in anticipation and mentally located the mother and little girl in the near darkness. In the silence that followed, everyone in the carriage became aware of a distant rumbling. Unease was replaced by a knowing malaise.

'Lift up the blind a little,' the man opposite said. With the light off, the old cow lifted the blind and the flickering orange glow was clear to see right across the horizon; vivid white flashes danced into the night sky.

'Oh goodness, Exeter is taking another hammering,' said the old cow. They sat in the semi-dark and their thoughts drifted to the poor unfortunate city-folk who were on the receiving end of another Blitz.

'Oh those poor, poor people,' said the companion. The Stranger smirked at their misplaced sympathies. You haven't seen anything yet, he thought to himself, I promise you that.

The smirk was quickly wiped from his face as the compartment door slid open and a torch flashed around the carriage. The man in the brown tweed coat stepped in.

The torch focused immediately on the Stranger.

'Can I see your papers please, sir?' said the man.

Every muscle in his body tightened. OK, here we go, he thought, plan A or plan B? He pulled his papers from an inside pocket with his left hand and passed them over as nonchalantly as he could and with his friendliest of smiles; but it was without emotion. The man in the tweed coat shone the torch on the papers, and back to the Stranger.

'Would you mind coming with me, sir?' he said. 'I'll hold onto these for now. Oh, and bring all your belongings.'

4

The Stranger weighed up his immediate options. As he stood up, he could have grabbed the mother and little girl but decided that as the train was stationary he'd take his chances outside the compartment. He donned his Fedora, pulled the leather suitcase from the rack and, as he squeezed past his fellow passengers, he snatched the little girl's sandwich and jammed it in his mouth. She looked horrified and burst into tears.

'Oh well I never did, I knew there was something bad about him,' said the old cow in a loud and knowing voice for all to hear. 'He looks foreign.'

He thrust his right hand back in his pocket and was tempted to stick the old cow, but followed the tweed coated man up the corridor. A single policeman fell in behind him. Now where's the other one? he wondered. He really needed to know that.

It took everyone by surprise. Without warning the train lurched forward, the Stranger feigned a stumble and the policeman behind him instinctively grabbed his left arm to steady him. In that split second he turned and the stiletto sank into the policeman's chest and was twisted with precision. The man's eyes bulged, his mouth fell open, but there was not a sound; he was dead before he hit the floor. The Stranger turned, half kneeling, coiled like a snake ready to strike. The man in the brown tweed coat turned, saw the policeman fall and he reached for the Webley snub-nosed pistol on his belt, but the stiletto was faster and slid effortlessly into his heart, followed by the practised twist. Staring into the cold, steel-grey eyes of the Stranger, he fell to his knees and then toppled forward face-down on the floor with a thud.

With speed and agility, the Stranger wiped the knife on the brown tweed coat, pocketed the gun, grabbed his identification papers and his brown leather suitcase, pulled down the adjacent door window, reached out, turned the door handle and disappeared into the night.

The train was three miles east of Exeter in the county of Devon.

Chartwell House, Kent

A cloud of scented cigar smoke wafted from the red leather high-backed chair in front of the roaring log fire. The smoker coughed, then grunted, and another billow of smoke erupted. His eyes were glued to the papers in his hand, trying to take in the enormity of the message. After several minutes he glanced up at the tall, well groomed officer standing next to him: Colonel Julian Bonham-Johns.

Born at the end of WWI, he never knew his father, Brigadier Sir Henry Bonham-Johns, who was killed at Locquignol in northern France one week before the end of the war. He had, however, followed in his father's footsteps, being commissioned into the Dorsetshire Regiment in 1930. As a young officer he spent several years in India and saw bloody action in the Waziristan campaign against the fierce tribal uprising. His outstanding ability to plan and organise men and materials in the remote mountainous region bordering Afghanistan resulted in him being transferred to the Special Operations Executive at the start of WWII. His initial role had been to train and support the fledgling French Resistance.

Churchill looked back at the papers on his lap.

'Can this be true, Julian?' he asked in his gruff voice. 'It simply flies in the face of all the intelligence we have. Eighty-eight men of bomber command sacrificed to destroy this target; brave boys all of them. Eleven Lancasters from 78 Squadron lost. Why, Julian? What's happening here?'

'Well, sir, it's not clear but it would seem—' but he was immediately interrupted.

'Damn it, Julian, "it's not clear" is not bloody good enough. Eighty-eight of our boys sacrificed, parents, wives and loved ones bereaved, not to mention the children who are fatherless, and you say "it's not clear"?'

The cat looked up from his basket by the fire and then flopped back down again. The awkward silence lasted many seconds as he took further deep puffs on his fast-dwindling cigar. The only sound was the crackling of the logs on the fire.

'You were saying, Julian?' he said in a more composed manner.

'Mr Churchill, the Kriegsmarinewerft in Wilhelmshaven is one of the most heavily defended locations in Germany. We estimate there are more than a thousand Flak anti-aircraft batteries in the area. Many of them the latest model, capable of pumping out deadly rounds to a height of twenty-five thousand feet, higher than our Lancasters can fly with a full bomb load. The fire power is truly overwhelming. It was a miracle that two Lancasters made it back to tell the story.'

'But Julian, the aerial photos show the Tirpitz seriously damaged, yet our on-the-ground intelligence suggests she's undamaged.'

Bonham-Johns cleared his throat and swallowed hard; he was not looking forward to this bit.

'Sir, we believe the pictures we took were of a decoy.' His throat closed and his voice faltered. Churchill glared at him in utter disbelief, and another plume of smoke erupted. There was a further silence.

'What about a drink, Julian? I have a rather fine Hine cognac or a single malt from the Isle of Skye for moments like this?'

'Yes please, sir. A Scotch, if I may,' Bonham-Johns croaked trying to find his voice; he could do with some liquid lubrication, not to mention liquid courage.

Churchill poured a large measure. 'Water or soda?'

'Water please, sir, just a dash.'

'Good man, just how it's supposed to be taken. I'm a cognac man myself.' He passed the glass to Bonham-Johns, poured himself a Hine cognac and sat back in his leather chair.

'You were saying, Julian?'

Bonham-Johns took a swig of the whisky and felt the warmth flow into his chest and revive his dry throat. He thought for a few seconds regarding the logic of what he was about to say.

'Mr Churchill, the aerial reconnaissance took place nearly thirty-six hours after the raid. 78 Squadron was over the target at 11 pm last Saturday, on Sunday we had no visibility over the target, and it was only yesterday morning at 9 am that the photo was taken.' He cleared his throat. 'It clearly shows a damaged ship that we thought was Tirpitz – that the Germans want us to think is Tirpitz – but if you look across to the other side of the harbour, can you see a large warehouse? But look at the location.'

Churchill lifted a magnifying glass to the photo and studied it carefully. 'I see it but—' he paused, 'my God, Julian, it's in the harbour, not on the dockside.'

'Exactly, sir. We think it's Tirpitz under camouflage. They moved her before the raid and put a mock-up in the old location. It's almost certainly further evidence that she's close to commissioning.'

'Julian, are you telling me we lost eighty-eight brave boys trying to blow up a bloody model?' Sparks and ash accompanied the explosion of smoke from his cigar. 'This is just unbelievable. It's a bloody catastrophe, Julian. The German Chancellor will be swigging schnapps and toasting our sheer bloody stupidity.'

Bonham-Johns thought Churchill was about to have a heart attack. The cat looked up again, disturbed by the commotion.

There was a knock at the drawing room door.

'What is it?' barked Churchill impatiently. The door opened and his wife, Clementine, appeared.

'Ah, Clemmie my love, do come in. I don't think you've met Colonel Julian Bonham-Johns?'

'Welcome to Chartwell,' she said, walking across the room and giving him a warm handshake.

'Clemmie, Julian is with the Special Operations Executive and has been appointed my Personal Operations Liaison Officer. He was two years below our Randolph at Eton.'

'Oh, you know Randolph?' she asked.

'Yes indeed, Mrs Churchill, we were in the Rugby XV together, but just for one season.'

'Randolph is off to North Africa shortly with the Hussars,' she said.

'Now, now Clemmie, loose talk and all that,' retorted Churchill.

'My dear, is your Operations Liaison Officer not to be trusted with such information?' said Clemmie, giving Bonham-Johns a cheeky wink. 'I wanted to ask if you will be staying for dinner tonight? I do hope so,' she added.

'No, Clemmie,' replied Churchill before Bonham-Johns could answer, 'Julian has important work to attend to; would you please excuse us, my dear?'

As she turned to go, she looked over her shoulder and said, 'I know when I'm not wanted.' It was said in a hangdog tone, but her warm smile suggested otherwise.

When the door closed behind her, Churchill walked across the drawing room, threw the finished cigar in the fire and took a new one from the box on the mahogany sideboard; he clipped it and lit it with a large silver lighter.

'Julian, you don't, do you?' he said, pointing at the cigar.

'No thank you, sir.'

Churchill walked to the window and pulled back one of the heavy, red velvet curtains. There was a long, reflective silence.

'Julian, you haven't seen the view from here on a fine day, have you? The most wonderful, spectacular view across the Weald of Kent. Nowhere am I happier than here, and yet, just over that horizon, Julian, Hitler and his Nazi thugs are plotting and scheming; they have designs on our green and pleasant land; they're so close I can smell them. We had the ultimate military disaster at Dunkirk back in June, but this is surely the lowest ebb. We know that German codebreakers have cracked our messages to Iceland and America, and this has resulted in more than two million tons of Atlantic Convoy shipping being sunk. We've lost HMS Ark Royal and three cruisers in the last four weeks alone, and that's before Tirpitz comes on the scene. We've got to destroy that beast, Julian. Our very survival on this island depends on it.'

He closed the curtain and turned towards Bonham-Johns.

'Julian, I want you to take personal control of this operation, and I want a plan and the intelligence to support it in one week. We need a code name. What would you suggest?'

'Sir, what about Operation Harpoon? We'll stalk her, attack her and kill her just as the old-time whalers did,' offered Bonham-Johns.

'Operation Harpoon it is, my boy,' replied Churchill.

Bonham-Johns smiled for the first time that afternoon.

'But remember, in wartime the truth is so precious that she should always be attended by a bodyguard of lies,' added Churchill, 'and Julian, not a word of this bombing catastrophe must get out, do you hear? Not a word. We need to apply the first of our diversionary bodyguards. Our brave and spirited citizens already have enough bad news to contend with.'

'Yes, sir, we'll close it down.'

'So what the hell are we going to do to neutralise the Tirpitz, Julian?'

'Well, sir, we do have some further options to consider.'

'That's what I like to hear. Tell me more, my boy. Another whisky?'

Tuesday 16 December 1941 – 6.00 pm

Telegraph Station, Porthcurno, Cornwall

At twenty-three, Robert Chenoweth was the youngest of the duty managers at the underground facility. Before the war, he had started his apprenticeship in the original Telegraph Station, following in the footsteps of his father Ross who was then manager. With the wartime transfer of skilled staff to other stations around the globe, promotion for Robert had come quickly but deservedly.

His shift had started at 5 am and it had been particularly busy with just over sixty thousand words an hour being processed for international distribution. He was tired, very tired. Due to the highly demanding work carried out by the cipher and transmission team in the instrument room, they were scheduled to work a maximum of twelve hours a day. British national security and that of the Allies and the Commonwealth depended upon quick and accurate work, sifting the important from the routine. The Telegraph was deemed so crucial that the Government had funded the mining of the new underground facility using the skills of the local Cornish tin miners. It had taken two years to construct, and they had moved in just four months earlier.

It was located on the very remote south-western tip of Cornwall, and getting technical reinforcements from other parts of the country was a logistical nightmare. German bombing had caused significant disruption to the Great Western Railway system, their main lifeline to the rest of the country. As a result, they were continually short staffed and had to work long hours to make up.

'OK,' said Robert, glancing at his watch, 'I'm going to get some shut-eye and I'll be back again at 10pm. If you have any priority conflicts speak with Josh Tregembo. Josh, keep this rabble on their toes, no shirking,' said Robert, to loud jeers and half-hearted insults.

It was a tight-knit and friendly team; they came from all four corners of the country. Robert, Josh and two others were locals; the remainder had been drafted in. Josh had been recently seconded from nearby RAF Sennen, which was the westernmost coastal Early Warning Radar Station and air base. Josh was a radio transmission specialist and known affectionately as Rusty due to his shock of ginger hair.

Robert left the instrument room, got his coat and lunch bag from his locker and walked down the concrete-lined tunnel towards the exit and the first checkpoint.

'Door B opens in two minutes,' said the guard, an army sergeant with a Smith and Wesson .45 revolver prominently positioned on the front of his belt.

Security of the facility was taken very seriously. Even though Robert had worked there for four years, since the war started he always felt under suspicion.

'Watch your step out there, lad,' said the sergeant, 'it's as slippery as hell.'

Robert said nothing and just watched the clock.

The sergeant lifted the phone and yelled, 'Door B open in one minute.'

A momentary silence, and then at the other end, 'All clear, Door A locked.'

With that, the sergeant activated the internal door lock and started to push. It took all his effort to inch open the heavy steel door. A red roof-mounted light flashed as the door slowly opened. Robert stepped through to a waiting area between the two doors. As Door B banged shut and the locks clanked in place behind him, he again waited. With the same fanfare, the second guard opened Door A from the outside and Robert stepped out into a blast of freezing cold air.

From the underground tunnel entrance he walked through a concrete-lined cutting covered in camouflage netting and out to the first security checkpoint and showed his papers. Robert was always amazed at how many different security guards were posted. He'd see the same one for a week or two and then wouldn't see them again for weeks, if at all.

Further on, he approached the gate in the twenty-foot-high electrified security fence and was let through. Again there was a control system that required one gate to be locked before the other could be opened. He showed his pass one more time as he exited the second gate. He lifted his coat collar up around his ears against the chill wind. There was one more security check point but this was guarded by bored conscripted soldiers and he was nodded through with little interest.

As Robert walked up the street, the army guards were changing shift. Sandbagged emplacements were manned by half-frozen, red-nosed soldiers rubbing their hands, looking forward to the end of shift and a hot meal and steaming mug of cocoa. Machine guns pointed up and down the road and across the valley. Nothing was quite as it seemed. Camouflage nets, painted structures, misleading signs and fake trees worked to mask the true identity of the area. Even the local hayricks were not what they seemed.

He walked up the road past the building with the big Bus Stop sign on the roof and on towards Boscarn Hamlets. It was a steep climb, and as he reached his house he was out of breath.

He unlocked the front door and made his presence known with a 'Hello I'm home.'

'Hello, sweetie,' said Megan, his wife. 'Would you like a cuppa and a bite to eat?' she asked, putting her arms around his neck and giving him a kiss on the lips.

'Oh, you do smell nice and you're so warm and—'

'Now, now. A cuppa is what's on offer,' she teased, pushing him away with a smile.

'Yes please, I'm just going to splash my face and lie down.'

'That's fine, I'll bring it up. Keep the noise down – May is asleep.'

When she entered the bedroom five minutes later, Robert was fast asleep and snoring.

Wednesday 17 December 1941 – 2.30 pm

Reykjavik, Iceland

Fifteen hundred miles north-west of Porthcurno, US Navy Rear Admiral Leonard Thornton gripped his seat tightly, his knuckles white with the effort. He was a seasoned warrior but only a fair-weather flyer and this was far from fair weather. He could happily stand on the bridge of a destroyer in a force eleven storm with sixty-foot waves breaking over the ship's bow but hated turbulence on a plane, especially over water. He'd never quite reconciled that.

Thornton had been handpicked for his new role by Chester Nimitz, Commander-in-Chief, U.S. Naval Fleet. The United States had declared war on Japan and Germany just ten days before, and he was detailed to fly to Pearl Harbour to join the Pacific Campaign. When he'd been summoned to the Pacific Fleet Headquarters in San Diego Bay, California, he'd expected a senior operational posting. However, he soon found out that Nimitz had a different idea.

'It's one of the most important naval roles in the Atlantic war according to President Roosevelt,' said Nimitz. 'We have been supplying our British Allies with critical supplies by sea for the last two years and now we need to support the Russians who have started a second front against the Germans. We need to supply them with arms and the latest munitions from the US via the North Atlantic to Archangel and Murmansk in Arctic Russia. These convoys get assembled in Iceland and then, with as much naval support as the Allies can muster, set sail around the north of the island and across the Arctic Sea. I need the best planning and logistics man available to coordinate these convoys and prioritise military support between us and the Brits – and that's you, Leonard. This is a mission-critical role.'

Oh God damn it, thought Thornton, knowing exactly what was coming, and, more to the point, he wasn't going to be based in his home state of Hawaii, where his wife and family lived.

The US Air Force Dakota in which Thornton found himself

bounced and bumped through low cloud on its final approach. The passengers all stared out into the blinding white cloud, all seeking the reassurance of seeing land beneath them. The engines eased back and the plane lurched lower, bouncing all the while; lower and lower and then full throttle, and the plane climbed steeply and banked. The pilot looked back through the open cockpit door and yelled his apology.

'Sorry, sir, there's a bit of a squall and we don't have visuals; don't want to end up in the pond, I'll try again.' Thornton's right leg started to tremble.

The Dakota banked around and flew back out to sea and then turned again for a second approach. Easing lower and lower, the plane bounced in the strong, gusty wind and then, one hundred feet below, an angry sea appeared. The plane levelled out and flew just below the cloud ceiling, bucking and bouncing all the while.

'I'll kiss the God-damn ground if we get down safely,' he vowed to himself.

Snow-covered land appeared beneath the plane, then the runway, and they were down, the plane bouncing and lurching from side to side.

As they taxied in, the pilot looked back and said, 'Sorry about the bumpy landing, sir. It's a bit blowy today.'

Cheerful little shit, thought Thornton, his heart still thumping and his right leg trembling. The five-hour flight from Halifax, Nova Scotia had been a nightmare for him.

His leg was still shaking as he climbed down the steps and saluted the pilot. 'Thank you, captain,' he said without a trace of his inner turmoil, 'is it always this rough up here?'

'Only for eleven-and-a-half months of the year, sir,' he replied with a broad grin.

The pilot was right: it was blowy, and driving snow whipped across the runway in sheets and stung his cheeks. It was bitterly cold. He strode over to the waiting jeep and jumped in.

'Make sure my kit is loaded,' he said to the driver.

'Sir, it'll be taken straight to your hut,' the driver replied.

'Christ, on top of this I'm going to spend my war in a fricking hut,' he mumbled to himself.

After a security check at the gate, the jeep sped off down the road. In the fast-fading daylight he saw a sign that read: 'Welcome to Valley Forge, home of Santa Claus'. Oh shit, he thought to himself.

'What the hell is Valley Forge?' he asked the driver.

'Sir, it's the US nickname for the Hvalfjörður Base. It's named after Valley Forge near Philadelphia, the military camp of the American Continental Army over the winter of 1777–1778. Nearly two-and-half thousand soldiers froze or starved to death. It's not quite so bad here. At least there's plenty of salt fish to eat,' he added, trying to be humorous.

Thornton, already depressed, now hit rock-bottom and shook his head.

'I've got to spend my war living in a hut in this godforsaken icebox eating salt fish. This is going to be a fricking nightmare!' he mumbled.

Wednesday 17 December 1941 – 3.00 pm

Cabinet War Rooms, London

Julian Bonham-Johns arrived at the Horse Guards Road entrance of the Cabinet War Rooms in a black Humber saloon. He entered the building, saluted the guards and walked down two flights of stairs. He then turned right through the sand-bagged doorway into the MI5 wing and headed straight to the meeting room. Two figures in military uniform were seated at a small mahogany desk, poring over a pile of papers.

'Ah, glad you could make it,' said Bonham-Johns, addressing Brigadier Cliff Latcham, Head of Counter Espionage for British Intelligence.

'Julian can I introduce you to Captain Montague Travis, he's from the Radio Security Service based in Arkley View in Barnet,' said Latcham. 'Thank you for your time, Julian. I wanted to alert you to a potentially serious situation that is unfolding.'

'Yes, go ahead,' replied Bonham-Johns and sat down opposite them straightening his tie and brushing back his jet-black hair with his fingers.

'Julian, you'll be aware that the Nazi Intelligence Agency, Abwehr, have an active espionage campaign against us in Britain. It involves the recruitment and training of dozens of spies, mostly of European nationalities with a few international types thrown in for good measure. More sinister is the recruitment of Nazi sympathisers in mainland Britain as "sleepers". Indeed, he has them in all our Commonwealth countries. These are spies living in villages, towns and cities that are seemingly part of our society, just like your average neighbour next door. The sleeper cells have been one of Colonel Canaris's most successful initiatives and, quite frankly, they're a thorn in our side.

'Now, our experience is that a few agents, only the most important ones, have Morse transmitters for sending coded messages. Montague's team have picked up one such message between an operative and the Abwehr listening post in Holland. The boffins in Bletchley believe the encrypted message is from an

17

Agent Banjo and reads "stiletto late stop awaiting contact stop could delay cutthroat stop inform violin."

'So what on earth does that mean?' queried Bonham-Johns.

'Well, it seems we have an Agent Banjo on the ground – with a transmitter, so they must be important – who is perhaps expecting Agent Stiletto who's been delayed, and there's at least one other in the ring, Agent Violin. Now we've come across the code name Cut-Throat before and it has been used by the Germans communicating with their Naval HQ in Trondheim, Norway. They refer to it as Operation Cut-Throat. We're pretty sure it's associated with the commissioning and assignment of Tirpitz from Wilhelmshaven, hence I thought you needed to know. The problem is that the transmission was so short we couldn't locate it. West of Bristol is the closest we can get.'

Latcham sat back to let Bonham-Johns absorb the information.

'What could possibly be the link with Tirpitz and the West Country?' asked Bonham-Johns with a furrowed brow.

'Well, whoever the team members are they must be planning something big and it might involve even more Agents, but at this time we're still trying to find out their true identities and what their target is.'

'West of Bristol is still a huge area, Cliff,' said Bonham-Johns, and Latcham nodded.

'Yes it is, but we do, however, have one possible lead. One of my Special Branch officers and a policeman were killed on a westbound train two days ago, just east of Exeter. A third policeman with them says they were in the process of detaining a suspected foreign agent. A search of the area was made but he'd disappeared into the night. So we know where this agent was two days ago, and the fact that he had to jump from the train means that he was delayed from his original plan. And he stabbed my man and the policeman with a thin double-bladed knife, so it appears Agent Stiletto is aptly named, assuming he's the same person,' added Latcham.

'The reason I wanted to alert you is that this points to their interest being not just west of Bristol but west of Exeter, and if it is associated with Tirpitz it's likely to be a naval target, so it's probably Devonport Dockyard or maybe one of the other high-security targets in the south-west, possibly Falmouth. We just don't have anything more specific at the moment,' Latcham added apologetically.

'So where do we go from here?' asked Bonham-Johns.

Latcham looked at Captain Montague Travis with a nod.

'Sir, we're putting in place additional monitoring across the southwest. We're using amateur radio hams to support us,' Travis's voice tailed off with the rather ridiculous-sounding concept, but he continued. 'These Voluntary Interceptors, VIs for short, are particularly adept at reading weak Morse transmissions in their area. When three or more VIs pick up a signal, we're able to triangulate the transmission location. The more VIs that pick up the signal, the more accurately we're able to calculate the location.'

'So are you saying we have amateur radio hams scattered around the countryside with radio sets?' asked Bonham-Johns.

'Oh no, sir. They had to hand in their transmitters but were able to keep their receivers. We have just increased the number of VIs in the southwest to thirty-two. That's more than twice the coverage we had before, and we're actively adding more each day,' Travis added with confidence.

'That's good, but what about Agent Violin, the other one? Where's he based?' asked Bonham-Johns.

'Julian, he's mentioned in many of the messages but doesn't appear to transmit. More of a receiver than a sender, probably communicates by phone or by written message to another agent,' said Latcham.

'So no idea of the location?' said Bonham-Johns, persisting with the line of questioning.

'Sorry, Julian, nothing at the moment, but we have it as a priority.'

'Well, thank you for bringing this to my attention, Gentlemen. I want to be kept fully informed of any further word from Stiletto or any of his musical friends,' said Bonham-Johns as they departed. 'Thanks for the briefing, Cliff, I'll keep Churchill informed. Oh, and on another subject, who do we have on the ground in Norway? I'm going to need some help over there, probably in the Trondheim area.'

'We do have Malmvig, Agent Aurora, over there but let me check the location and status and I'll get right back to you,' replied Latcham, and with a handshake, he and Travis left the room.

Bonham-Johns remained in the conference room to write a brief on what he'd just learned. As he thought about the implications of the Nazi agent network, he rubbed the scar above his left eye. Twenty minutes later when he'd finished, he took the document to Patricia Wade, head of the typing pool.

'Pat, this to Sir Alistair for the attention of The Boss, pronto please.'

As he backed out of the cramped office he bumped into a young brunette carrying a tray of crockery and he grabbed her shoulders to help regain her balance.

'I'm so sorry,' she said, 'how careless of me, I really should look where I'm going.'

'No, not at all. It's entirely my fault,' said Bonham-Johns.

Balancing the tray between her hip and left arm, she offered her right hand and said, 'I'm Lucy. Pleased to meet you I'm sure.'

'Likewise,' said Bonham-Johns and shook her hand. It was soft and warm, and she held the grip for a touch longer than necessary.

'And you are?' she asked with her head to one side.

'Oh, yes, sorry, Bonham-Johns, uh, Julian,' he said.

'You're new around here, aren't you? What do you do?' she asked.

Bonham-Johns was immediately on the defensive.

'If I told you that, Lucy, I'd have to kill you, and I don't want to do that. Who'd make the tea around here?' He said it with a serious look on his face but she smiled as they parted. Bonham-Johns was taken aback by the surprise intimacy of the moment.

Thursday 18 December 1941 – 11.15 am

Penzance, Cornwall

The Cornish fishing town of Penzance is the western terminus of the Great Western Railway. On this late December morning there was bright sunshine, but a keen wind sent white horses galloping across Mounts Bay. The first daffodils nodded bright yellow in the park, now having second thoughts about blooming so early. It had been a warm start to the month but had turned unseasonably cold for an area usually known as The Cornish Riviera.

Clara Chenoweth walked down Market Jew Street right into the face of the east wind, holding onto her hat in the fierce gusts. Her chubby cheeks, usually rosy red, were purple and her nose was going blue. 'Bugger this for a game of soldiers,' she muttered under her breath. Within a few steps she turned into Blewett's the Drapers and the doorbell chinged behind her.

'Ullow Jane, how's you my love?' she said to the shop assistant in her broad Cornish accent.

'Oh you know, can't grumble thanks Clara, how are you, haven't seen you for ages, how's Ross and Bert and the family?'

'Everyone's OK,' said Clara, 'Ross is still overseas with the Telegraph and Bert is out all hours with the home guard and I'm some worried for him now winter's 'ere. Always chesty, he is. He still desperately misses his Val. She's been gone near eighteen months now.'

'Oh I know, so sad, and how's Robert and Megan?'

'Of course you won't know will you? Megan's had a baby girl, May, eight pounds ten ounces.'

'Ohhh, congratulations, Granny, what a lovely Christmas present.'

'Course Robert spends all hours down at the Telegraph,' said Clara, looking pensively around the shop to see if anyone was listening. 'Lots of activity goin' on, soldiers all over, can't say nothing mind, but lots 'appening. There's a young captain goes to our church, very 'ansome, looks just like Clark Gable in uniform.' She chuckled out loud at the thought.

21

'Ohhh, you must introduce me,' said Jane. 'Now, what can I do for you?'

'Well I want some pink ribbon for the cardie I'm knittin' little May.'

Jane rummaged in a drawer and pulled out a roll.

'Just two foot will be fine,' said Clara.

'That's tuppence, please,' said Jane, handing Clara the package, 'and don't forget to invite me down to meet your soldier boy some time.'

'Oh you'll 'ave to wait your turn while Ross is away,' Clara chuckled, and saying her goodbyes she left the warmth of the shop and headed out into the cold and blowy street.

The bright sunshine had been replaced by a veil of high cloud that made it feel even colder. She struggled back up the hill with her bulky frame trying to hold her back and with a big sigh of relief turned into Opie's the Chemist. She bought some cod liver oil for her father-in-law, Bert, and then on up to the Star Hotel to pick up something she'd ordered. Whilst she tried to ignore the temptation she decided to have a cup of tea and a sticky bun; just to keep off the cold, she told herself.

'Right raw today,' she said to the waitress, 'it's come in cloudy, and wouldn't be surprised if we don't get snow.'

Clara slumped in the chair with a big sigh.

'Oh, me feet and me knees,' she complained, 'cuppa please, me dear, and one of your treats.'

The young girl brought a pot of tea with a little milk jug.

'Sorry, missus, there's no sugar today.'

'Oh, not to worry,' said Clara, 'it's the same all over.'

Clara had just taken the first bite of her bun when down in the harbour the air raid sirens started to wail. Almost immediately there was the loud chatter of anti-aircraft fire and in the same instant planes roared overhead, canons rattling, followed seconds later by two huge explosions. Everything in the tea room shook, crockery dropped and smashed and the chandelier swung wildly in the ornate ceiling. Shouts and screams erupted in the chaos. Clara fell sideways off her chair and landed heavily on the floor.

'Oh shit, me bloody backside!' she cried as the waitress tried to lift her bulky frame. She struggled in vain and had to get the help of another waitress to lift her up. Clara was badly shaken.

'Oh bugger me backside 'urts,' she spluttered, rubbing it hard with her left hand.

Looking out the window there was pandemonium: fire wardens rushing down the street and an ambulance, bell ringing insistently, weaving through the scattered debris.

'Oh bugger,' she said, 'look, I landed on me treat!' But she wasn't going to waste it, and she popped what remained in her mouth. She reached for her cup of tea, ignoring the dust floating on top, and quickly drank it.

Someone ran in from the street and yelled, 'Jerry's hit the train station, and we need all able-bodied men down there immediately.'

'Oh Lordy,' said Clara, 'I 'ope the bus is still going, I must rush.'

'Will you be alright, missus? Can I help you?' enquired the waitress.

'No, no my love, I'll be fine.'

As Clara left, the waitress handed her a small wrapped parcel.

'Your sister Rhoda left this for you,' she added.

'Oh thanks, I nearly forgot that,' said Clara, and painfully limped out of the hotel.

Out on the street she was shocked to see the damage and how close it had come to the hotel. Palls of smoke rose from the railway station at the bottom of the road, and the opposite side of Market Jew Street was strewn with broken glass, bits of timber and stonework. She thought about Jane in the Drapers and limped back down the hill as fast as she could. To Clara's relief, Jane was out on the pavement broom in hand, sweeping away the broken glass.

'Jane,' yelled Clara, 'are you alright my love?'

'By the Grace of God, Clara, I was out the back putting the kettle on. What about you?'

'Oh I fell on me backside but fortunately there's a lot of padding there. I'll survive,' she said.

Clara waved and walked gingerly but as quickly as she could back up the hill, limping with her badly bruised buttock. She shuddered to think that if she had left Blewett's the Drapers ten minutes later she would have been on that side of the street during the attack.

She just wanted to get out of this nightmare and retreat to her cosy, quiet, safe home and her family. Big tears ran down her cheeks with the emotion. At the top of the street she saw a group of people by the Humphrey Davy statue. Rivulets of blood were clearly visible running down the road. As she got closer she deliberately averted her gaze but couldn't resist a quick glance not knowing what to expect, but to her mixed relief it was a horse, lying prostrate, still attached to its cart. It had been tied up outside the Market House and had been hit by the strafing. She looked away, feeling quite unwell. At least someone will have fresh meat for Christmas, she thought, as she limped on up the hill with her buttock throbbing.

Ten minutes later and exhausted, she reached the bus station and was relieved to see the familiar Pascoe's bus and Vivian Thomas the driver.

'The buggers near got me, Viv,' she said gasping for breath. 'Goin' about me Christmas shoppin' and the buggers take a potshot at me, tisn't right, the buggers,' her nervous emotions turning into a tirade.

'Twas a cross-channel raider group, two Heinkels,' said Viv. 'Me son Alan saw 'em, said they near knocked the chimney pots off up Heamoor. Come on, Clara, let me help you up.'

With much pushing and grumbling she struggled onto the bus and sat gingerly in a window seat. The other passengers she'd come up with that morning started to arrive and were chattering frenetically about their experiences. Lots of head-shaking, tut-tutting and near-miss stories. They were all traumatised. The war usually seemed so far from West Cornwall, almost unreal apart from the rationing. And then there it was, suddenly and unexpectedly in their midst. It was terrifying.

'They took Evelyn Varcoe to 'ospital,' said one of the passengers, 'she got hit by flying glass.'

'Oh, poor Evie,' said someone else.

'Switch on the engine, Viv, and let's get some heat going, it's

24

bloody freezing back 'ere,' said the man in front of Clara.

Even though petrol rationing meant Viv had to be very sparing with fuel, his passengers needed some comfort today and he started the engine and put the heater dial to maximum. Even so, he wasn't convinced it would make much difference.

After waiting a further ten minutes for the stragglers, Viv Thomas finally engaged a crunching first gear as the first snowflakes started to scud past the bus. He switched on the wiper and looked gloomily at the threatening purple sky. As he pulled off, there was a loud banging on the side of the bus. He stopped, opened the door, and a man got on. He walked back to the one empty seat next to Clara, put his brown leather, weather-beaten suitcase in the rack above and sat down.

Thursday 18 December 1941 – 5.45 am

Hvalfjörður, Iceland

The snow squeaked beneath his Arctic combat boots as Rear Admiral Leonard Thornton walked across the yard to the operations room. After the traumatic flight of yesterday he'd been dog-tired and had forgone being hosted in the mess and had gone straight to bed. He'd slept like a log. His room in the new Nissen hut complex was warm and comfortable, a pleasant surprise. He was woken by the duty sergeant and had a refreshing shower and a warm and filling breakfast of waffles, crispy bacon and scrambled eggs; so good he'd had second helpings. He'd not fancied the cheese or pickled fish. Who the hell eats rancid fish for breakfast? he wondered. At 5.45 am he was heading to his first 6 am operations meeting.

Captain Dirk Kinnenberg was already at the chart table assessing the intelligence that had come in overnight. The table was twenty feet square and the map on it covered the whole of the North Atlantic from eastern Canada across to Archangel in Russia and down to the north coast of Spain. Small model ships of different colours were spread across the table, each one showing the last-known location of convoy ships, Allied naval vessels, German naval ships and U-boats.

Kinnenberg saluted as Thornton entered the chart room.

'Good morning, sir, welcome to the new Naval Operations Room at Hvalfjörður. I trust you had a good night?'

'Yes thank you, captain,' said Thornton, looking around the room with genuine interest. 'So, give me a rundown on what we have here.' His spiky, greying, crew cut hair gave him a rather menacing edge, Kinnenberg thought.

'Well, sir, this is a new base commissioned just last month. Here we coordinate the assembly and protection of all North Atlantic and Arctic convoys. President Roosevelt himself approved the construction of this facility back in June this year when he and Churchill signed the US–Icelandic defence agreement and the US took over the occupation of Iceland from the British.

In that time we've started to improve the port facilities, upgrade the marine repair service, and set up stockpiles of fuel, munitions, general provisions and military spares,' said Kinnenberg with pride. It had been his whole life for the last five months. 'It's good to hear Uncle Sam is making a difference,' said Thornton. 'And what about supporting the locals? I understand that's part of our mandate?'

'Sir, yes it is. In addition to fighting the war, we also have to supply the Icelanders with food and other essential supplies. Denmark, their historic motherland, is now under German control. It actually takes quite a lot of our time and resources because the locals are rather demanding and resentful. Not surprising really – their whole world has been turned upside down. But we have to keep them on-side because there are known to be German sympathisers and spies on the island, and we have to curb their influence.'

'They should be more grateful,' scowled Thornton. 'Perhaps we should leave them to starve and freeze in the dark,' he said, thinking of the Valley Forge analogy.

Kinnenberg was surprised by the bluntness and eyed the Rear Admiral with even more suspicion.

'What's this cluster of ships on the north of the island?'

'Sir, we have two ice-free fjords with ports, here at Hvalfjörður and that one at Eyafjord. We have made good progress at both locations fitting submarine and torpedo nets across the mouth of the fjords. This allows the convoys to assemble, refuel and carry out repairs in relative safety. We do have some exposure from the air particularly now that the Germans have air bases operational in Norway, but we're strengthening our anti-aircraft defences as well.'

Thornton leaned over the map and pointed. 'Why are all these vessels laying in Hvalfjörður? There must be forty ships here. If they're at anchor they're idle.'

'Yes, sir, we're holding more ships than usual because of a recent upturn in U-boat activity off the west coast. The U-boats are a real threat, sir, and have sunk a large tonnage of merchant shipping.'

'So what the hell are the Allies doing about it, and why isn't Uncle Sam out there kicking some Nazi butt?' Thornton asked.

'Well, sir, we have been. We had USS Kearny on patrol but she was torpedoed by a U-boat a few weeks back. She is still undergoing repair. The Brits are now also involved in the operation and to their credit have destroyed six U-boats in the last week alone. They've also succeeded in capturing one of the new type VIIC submarines, U-570, that was caught on surface by a Hudson aircraft from 269 Squadron. A pretty clever bit of work because the Germans usually scuttle them if they get caught. They got the crew, weapons and operating manuals. It's a real coup.'

'So it was a US plane that caught them,' said Thornton with a smile.

'Uh, yes, sir,' said Kinnenberg, not wishing to point out that whilst the Hudson was manufactured in the United States, 269 Squadron was in fact British.

'What's this collection of ships way over here?' asked Thornton.

'Sir, that's Scapa Flow, a protected body of water in the Orkney Islands, Scotland. It's about 120 square miles in area and is one of the great natural anchorages of the world. Actually, Viking ships anchored in Scapa Flow more than 1,000 years ago,' added Kinnenberg, rather proud of his knowledge of marine history. Thornton just grunted.

'From Scapa Flow, the Allies patrol the North Sea from the French coast in the south to Norway in the east and up to the Arctic Ocean in the north,' Kinnenberg continued. 'It's the hub of all Allied operations in that sector, even more important now that Norway has fallen. There are regular confrontations with German convoys resupplying their Expeditionary Force. The Brits have the Western Approaches covered from here out of Devonport, Plymouth on the southwest coast of England. That's the same port our forefathers . . . ' but he dried up. Thornton looked at him with a quizzical sneer; he didn't need to say anything. I'm going to have to watch this guy, thought Kinnenberg.

'So, captain, when are we going to get these convoys on their way to Archangel?'

'Sir, we have dispatched PQ6 to Murmansk, and the next two convoys will be combined as PQ7 and that will leave in five days. Returning Convoy QP4 has only just managed to get out of Archangel because the White Sea has frozen early this winter.'

'Captain, Archangel remains the priority port of destination. It's four hundred miles closer to the Russian front than Murmansk. From Murmansk the materials have to divert through St Petersburg. Surely the Russians have icebreakers to support the efforts of the Allies?'

'Yes they do, sir. The icebreakers Sadko and Lenin are stationed there but when the ice gets too thick even they can't forge a passage.'

I'll tell you what we're going to do, captain. Tell Archangel to have all available icebreakers ready to receive convoy PQ7 one week today – they sail in three days. Tell them there is a strategic cargo that is high priority for the Western Front, is that clear? We can't have our Russian comrades shirking their responsibilities because of a little ice, can we?' added Thornton.

Kinnenberg doubted the Rear Admiral had ever experienced pack ice and was about to comment but thought better of it. 'Yes, sir, that's clear,' he said.

He had a further seven months before he was scheduled for home leave, and that suddenly seemed an eternity.

Thursday 18 December 1941 – 2.00 pm

Pontchâteau, France

In pouring rain and winter gloom, Captain Hans Dettsmann stared out of the back of the Opel staff car as it crawled through the muddy potholed roads of the Pays de la Loire region of the Atlantic coast. He was a decorated soldier and proudly wore his iron cross. He'd had a private education, had excelled at sport at Kolleg Sankt Blasien and was an under eighteen boxing champion of Baden-Württemberg. From an early age he was an excellent marksman, having been taught by his Grandfather to hunt deer and wild boar in the Black Forest. His physical strength and leadership skills had been noted by the Nazi party and he was quickly enlisted into the elite Mountain Division. On graduation he had been posted to Hamburg where he had first met the members of his platoon.

Their first role had been to seek out and terminate resistance fighters in the Tatra Mountains in southeast Poland soon followed by deployment to Narvik ahead of the invasion of Norway. Dettsmann had been made platoon commander of twenty-five commandos who were dropped in the mountains above Narvik and had then destroyed the anti-aircraft facilities and finally captured the radio station. Dettsmann had shown outstanding bravery in rescuing one of his badly wounded soldiers; he carried him on his back for fifty yards whilst under enemy fire.

The staff car rattled and bounced over the potholed road. He was tired, hungry and thirsty. His flight from Hamburg had departed late because of Allied bombing, and the plane had then been diverted to Nantes due to bad weather. The twenty mile journey had been slow. Military convoys had forced them to pull off the road for more than an hour despite the driver waving his priority pass. More than anything he needed a drink, a strong drink.

After what seemed an eternity to Dettsmann, the car pulled up at a checkpoint in front of huge wrought iron gates. A flashlight flicked around the interior, passes were inspected and the gates opened and they were off again, sweeping up the drive to an imposing Chateau. The car crunched to a halt on the gravel drive in front of the main door. Security was tight with soldiers patrolling the front of the building and two armoured cars positioned either side of the drive.

The driver opened the door of the staff car, and Dettsmann got out and looked up, admiring the grandeur of the Chateau. The design was more subtle and pleasing to the eye than the equivalent castles in his homeland. He marched up the stone steps and the large iron-studded wooden door swung open before him, and he entered the grand entrance hall. Granite columns and a sweeping flight of stairs greeted him. To the right of the hall was a highly polished oak door and to the left a log fire roared in a large stone fireplace. He walked to the fire and rubbed his hands and felt the warmth flowing back; he hadn't realised how cold he'd got on the journey.

As he looked up he saw an SS Officer staring at him from across the hall. Another officious little Nazi obsessive, he thought as he walked across to him, deliberately straightening his Iron Cross.

'I'm Captain Dettsmann to see Admiral Raeder,' he said.

The officer, seeing the medal and his rank, saluted and pointed to the door. He knocked and went in.

A young and attractive Navy Auxiliary was sitting behind a large mahogany desk and she smiled warmly.

'I'll inform the Admiral you have arrived,' she said, and pointed to a black leather couch.

As the bus throbbed its way up the steep hill to Trelew Moor, snowflakes splattered thickly on the windscreen and Viv Thomas stared intently into the semi-dark trying to keep the bus in the middle of the snow-covered road.

'Don't like the look of this,' Clara said in a concerned voice to the Stranger beside her. 'You know, in the blizzard of 1891 the Penzance stagecoach got stuck up 'ere, and the horses and half the passengers froze to death.'

The Stranger said nothing and wished she'd shut up; his head was throbbing.

'Well you see,' continued Clara, 'it's supposed to have come in sudden like and caught everyone unawares. Have you got far to go?' He shook his head but said nothing.

'Where about's you goin' then?'

He didn't answer.

Oblivious to the snub, she carried on. 'Oh I lives up at Boscarn at the top end of the village, nice place, lovely neighbours. Bit crowded mind, six of us. Got the father-in-law Bert, son Robert, his wife Megan and little May, she's just four months. Oh yes, and then there's me hubby, Ross. He's overseas with the Telegraph.'

He's lucky, thought the Stranger, but he said nothing and just stared ahead. Won't she ever shut up?

'Oh I don't like the look of this snow. It'll take us longer to get back for sure, that's if we make it at all,' said Clara.

Oh shit, thought the Stranger, I can't take two hours of this, and pulled a hip flask from his inner jacket pocket and took a large swig.

'Oh that's a nasty gash on your forehead,' Clara remarked, 'you need to get that seen to. Did you get caught up in the bombing today?'

He nodded, thinking of the irony of being injured on the last day of his long journey.

'Those German fly boys near got me too,' she said indignantly.

'There I was going about me Christmas shoppin' and Bob's your uncle there's bombs and bullets all around. Ten minutes later and I wouldn't be here,' she said with feeling. 'Those Nazi buggers,' she added, 'and I 'urt me backside.'

The Stranger smiled to himself. *You're a pain in the backside in more ways than one, my dear.* Even with his head throbbing from the wound, he finally dozed off with Clara's chatter still buzzing in his ears.

After more than two hours of travelling, Viv Thomas pulled the bus into Porthcurno village square, and the passengers stood up stiffly and slowly exited the bus. The Stranger left quickly, rudely pushing in front of some of the passengers. Brown leather suitcase in hand, he quickly disappeared into the darkness.

He trudged through the thickly falling snow up the steep hill out of the village. He needed to take a track up past Polgassick Farm but decided to keep to the fields. It was pitch-black and several times he stumbled. Once he dropped the heavy leather case when he slipped into a ditch and it took him minutes to find it again. The deep snow leaked into his stout walking shoes and started to melt. *I could do without this crap,* he thought.

His head still throbbed from the gash on his forehead caused by a piece of flying debris at Penzance station that morning. He took the torch out of the case and went on his way using it sparingly. *Who the hell would be out on a night like this anyway?* he thought.

Ten minutes later he was getting concerned. He should have been at the farm but either he hadn't gone far enough or he'd missed it. He turned ninety degrees to his left to where he thought the farm track should be. A couple of minutes later he was relieved to hit a track and moments later he saw some dim lights where the farm should be.

He worked around the farm and headed off across the fields again. Thirty minutes later the snow had eased and the moon appeared fleetingly between scudding clouds. In one brief break he saw snow-covered houses and St Levan church nestled about half a mile away in the valley below. With a renewed spring in his step it took him a further fifteen minutes to reach the safe house arranged by his local contact.

Fern Cottage was conveniently situated just outside the hamlet and set amongst protective trees. He went around to the back door and searched for the key. It wasn't under the plant pot as he'd been told but he was afraid to use his torch. He took his gloves off and searched in the flower bed, his hands, already cold, were now numb. Was that it? No. Where the hell is it? he thought. Getting irritated, he went back to the flowerpot and searched underneath again. He'd missed the key the first time because it had frozen to the bottom of the pot.

He breathed on the key to melt the lump of ice, slid it into the lock and it turned with a reassuring click. He slipped in, cautiously and quietly closed the door and stood motionless, listening. He put the leather suitcase down and pulled out his trusty stiletto and with the torch in the other hand checked the entire house. Satisfied it was empty, he went out the front door and tied some thin twine across the path about one foot above the ground and did the same outside the back door. He needed to know if anyone was snooping around.

When he returned to the kitchen he checked the blackout, lit the oil lamp and started to relax for the first time in several days. He took off his coat, opened the stove door and gave the fire a good poke. The heat started to thaw his hands and despite the intense pain he smiled at a job well done, thus far. Gingerly he washed the wound on his head with cold water and patted it dry with a cloth; it was still throbbing painfully.

With circulation restored he put the kettle on the old black cast iron Cornish range and went to the larder cupboard to look for the provisions. As he tucked into spam, homemade pickle and bread he poured a cup of sweet black tea. It was such a treat to taste sugar again. His contact had done well, he thought.

The plan was coming together, stage one was complete. He'd reached his destination and he started to rehearse in his mind the clandestine activities of the next few days and his ultimate escape in eighteen days' time.

Thursday 18 December 1941 – 5.00 pm

Pontchâteau, France

Dettsmann was getting impatient; he had been kept waiting nearly fifty minutes, but the young Navy Auxiliary was the prettiest girl he'd seen in a long while and he couldn't help staring at her and imagining. She had held his gaze on several occasions and smiled. When she brought him coffee she had bent over him to put the cup on the table and he'd been tempted to touch her, but did nothing. Time passed by slowly. His daydream snapped when the phone on the desk rang loud and shrill.

'Show him in,' said the voice at the other end.

'Admiral Raeder will see you now,' the auxiliary said with another smile.

He knocked on the door, walked in and gave a salute in his crisp, meticulous manner.

'Captain Dettsmann reporting, sir.'

'You're late, Dettsmann, sit down,' said Raeder. 'Drink?'

'Yes please, sir,' but he thought the comment on his timing was a bit rich given the hour he'd been made to wait.

Dettsmann anticipated schnapps but the Admiral poured him a generous half-glass of cognac.

'Fortunately the Chateau comes well provisioned,' he said. 'They certainly know how to live well, these French.'

Dettsmann noted that the Admiral had filled his own glass almost to the top.

He glanced around the room; the walls were covered in tapestries and the heads of long-dead animals and light from the log fire danced around the ornate painted plaster ceiling. The Admiral sat in a chair the other end of the fireplace, both of them soaking up the radiant heat from the flames and the inner warmth provided by the cognac.

'Well, Dettsmann I hear you're something of a hero. Platoon leader in the Third Mountain Division, dropped behind the lines ahead of Operation Weserübüng; and then decorated. What did you do to win your Cross?' he asked without any real interest, just staring into the fire.

'Just my job, sir,' said Dettsmann rather brusquely; it was the Mountain Division's code not to boast. There was a silence and Dettsmann felt he needed to say more.

'We were dropped in the mountains above the Port of Narvik to disrupt their defences ahead of the invasion of Norway. We secured their radio communications station and captured their cipher operators and their codes.'

There was a further silence.

'Quite,' said Raeder, 'I'm familiar with the invasion. General von Falkenhorst, who planned it, is a good friend.' Dettsmann felt uneasy.

'Now then, Dettsmann, any idea why you're here?' asked Raeder.

'None at all, sir.'

'Let me fill you in then,' said the Admiral as he relaxed back in the chair.

'I'm Admiral Erich Raeder, the commander of the Kriegsmarinewerft. We have the best seamen and fighting ships in the world and we have brought the might of the British Navy to its knees. You'll have heard of my prize fleet of Battleships: the Scharnhorst, Graf Spee, Scheer, Gneisenau, Prinz Eugen and now nearing completion the mother of them all, the Tirpitz. You have heard of the Tirpitz?'

'Yes indeed, sir.'

He wanted to add that he knew she was the sister ship of the Bismarck. But the Bismarck had been sunk by the Allies back in May and he thought that would not go down well with the cantankerous, inebriated Admiral.

'Tirpitz,' he continued, 'is a game-changer that will help lead the Third Reich to glorious victory. She alone can challenge the naval might of the British Empire. She's over fifty thousand tons, top speed of thirty-five knots, has eight fifteen inch and twelve six inch guns. She can obliterate the enemy at fifteen miles and with her twelve inch thick steel hull she's impenetrable.'

'The master plan,' said the Admiral with relish, 'is to deploy

Tirpitz to Norway. She will attack Allied convoys bound for the Soviet Union so that we strangle those Soviet dogs of their lifeblood and starve the red scum and eradicate them from the earth. Tirpitz will harry the British fleet, help us invade Iceland and pave the way for the invasion of Britain. These will be glorious times. The Führer has agreed to this strategy and as we speak Tirpitz is undergoing final completion in Wilhelmshaven. She's invincible, Dettsmann, the greatest fighting machine on earth.' His eyes were popping and staring, trance-like.

The moment passed and he added, 'Captain Topp has informed me that she will be ready for combat operations within weeks. This will be one of the defining moments of the Third Reich,' he said with pride, his chest puffed out.

'Sir, I thought Tirpitz had been damaged by British bombing?' Dettsmann blurted out and immediately regretted it. The Admiral glared at him, took a large gulp of cognac and forced a steely smile.

'You're misinformed, Dettsmann,' he said acerbically. 'Whilst she's in dock she's been subject to some poorly planned and largely unsuccessful attacks by the remnants of the RAF. Recently a large raid failed to hit her at all,' he said with an obvious smirk. 'They missed her altogether,' and the smirk turned into a cackling laugh.

'No, Dettsmann, Tirpitz is undamaged and close to sailing. The Führer has given orders that she must be protected at all costs. We must protect her with every last drop of our blood.'

Dettsmann downed the last of his cognac and swallowed hard; he didn't like the sound of that. He was wondering why the Admiral was telling him about battleships. He was a special operations soldier.

Raeder reached for the cognac and topped up his glass. Dettsmann was not offered more.

'What role do you expect me to have in this, Admiral?' he asked.

Raeder stood up, walked a little unsteadily over to Dettsmann, leaned over and stared him in the face. He seemed to be searching for the words.

'I need some diversionary tactics,' Raeder said, 'and that's where you come in.'

Dettsmann went to take another swig but his glass was empty.

'I want you to select four of your best men for a commando-style raid, similar to the one you carried out at Narvik. It'll be the same objective, comparable terrain but a different location and this time you will go in by submarine. This is a high-security area and your arrival needs to be top secret. Be back here in thirteen days with your team fully operational and provisioned – that's the 31st.'

Dettsmann was about to ask for more detail but it was clear the meeting was over.

Friday 19 December 1941 – 7.00 am

Höfði House, Reykjavik, Iceland

Colonel Julian Bonham-Johns introduced himself to Rear Admiral Thornton and Captain Kinnenberg. Although outranked by Thornton, he had special orders that came right from the very top; he was effectively in charge of the meeting, much to Thornton's annoyance.

He had flown in from London the previous afternoon and had been given a room in the Höfði House Hotel in northern Reykjavik. It was the best accommodation in Iceland and boasted Churchill as one of its guests earlier in the year. After two years of blackout in London, Bonham-Johns had been elated to see the lights of Reykjavik from his room and he'd left the curtains open to relish it further. It might be a small city but there was something very reassuring in the normality of the twinkling lights.

The three met in the drawing room of the hotel. Tea, coffee and sandwiches were available, which again was a pleasant surprise given the wartime rationing in Britain.

'Rear Admiral, I have been sent here to debrief you and your team on an important development. I believe you should have correspondence from President Roosevelt to this effect?'

Thornton was floored by the whole thing. I've got a God damn Limey junior officer about to tell me what to do, he thought and just stared at the colonel. There was a pregnant pause.

'Quite,' said Bonham-Johns, realising that this wasn't going to be an easy meeting. He brushed his black hair back with his fingers.

'Gentlemen, let's sit around the table,' said Bonham-Johns, unrolling a map and pinning it down using the ashtrays. Thornton had never been referred to as a gentleman and he didn't like it.

'It's "sir" to you, colonel,' he said in a voice that cut the air. Kinnenberg sat opposite them at the table and contemplated the start of a US–British diplomatic crisis.

'Certainly, sir,' Bonham-Johns replied, completely unfazed.

'British Military Intelligence, MI1 the code-breaking depart-ment and MI14 the aerial reconnaissance and photography department, have been keeping an eye on the construction of the German battleship Tirpitz in Wilhelmshaven. Our cryptogra-phers have managed to break the Lorenz cipher codes used by the Germans and it is clear that they're getting ready for something big. The intercepted radio traffic indicates she's close to commis-sioning and preparing to make a break for it. It's just a matter of when, and sir, the Allies want to know when that is, and if at all possible influence that timing. This is critical.'

'Our detailed high-altitude pictures of the harbour confirm her status and for the first time we have an indication of her armaments and she is clearly one of the most potent battleships in the world,' added Bonham-Johns.

'A pity the bulk of the US battleship fleet is in the Pacific, or we'd sort out these Nazi tin cans in short order,' said Thornton with patriotism.

Bonham-Johns was tiring of Rear Admiral Thornton's rhetoric. He stared at the spiky-haired Rear Admiral.

'Sir, with respect, as of two weeks ago the biggest operational US battleships in the Pacific Fleet are either at the bottom of Pearl Harbour or out of action. As of now there's only one more powerful battleship than Tirpitz and that's Japan's Yamato, and that's in the Pacific,' he said in a controlled voice.

When he'd finished, Bonham-Johns glared at Thornton to bring the message home. Kinnenberg fidgeted with his hands.

Thornton was incandescent and his cheeks were bright red.

'Have you come here to insult the US Navy, the finest Navy in the world and the one that will help save your Limey asses you ungrateful little—' stopping himself just in time.

'Not at all, sir,' replied Bonham-Johns in a controlled, authori-tative voice. 'Just stating the facts and highlighting what a potent force the Tirpitz represents in the Atlantic and the critical impor-tance to the Allies, that's Britain and the USA, to hunt it down and destroy it, by whatever means.' Bonham-Johns emphasised the 'Britain and the USA', almost spitting the words out. After many seconds of staring eye to eye, Thornton looked away.

'Right,' Bonham-Johns continued, 'the air defences at Wilhelmshaven are so deadly Churchill has ruled out further bombing raids. That means we need to have a reception committee waiting for Tirpitz when she sails. Our intelligence suggests she's going to sail to Norway and then, based in one of the fjords, raid the North Atlantic and Arctic convoys. We are developing a military strategy that mobilises both naval and air assets, and running in parallel we will have a programme of misinformation. The latter will be multifaceted and it will have to be subtle but compelling. We are naming this Operation Harpoon and, Rear Admiral, we need your help in this. That was the essence of the message from President Roosevelt I believe?' he added for affect.

When Bonham-Johns had finished there was a long silence with just the hypnotic ticking of the Grandfather clock in the corner of the room.

'So what do you need from me?' asked Thornton.

'Sir, both naval assets and misinformation,' said Bonham-Johns.

'With respect to the latter I believe you have an Arctic Convoy scheduled to depart in the next few days, captain?'

'Yes, sir,' said Kinnenberg, 'Convoy PQ7 will be leaving for Archangel in two days.'

'Archangel?' queried Bonham-Johns.

'Yes, sir,' replied Kinnenberg in a hesitant voice.

'You do realise the White Sea has already frozen and is likely to be impassable?'

'Uhh, yes, sir,' said Kinnenberg, not daring to look at Thornton, 'but it remains the priority destination and we have alerted the Russians to have all available icebreakers on station.'

'Right,' said Bonham-Johns, not at all convinced.

'What's the total complement and how many foreign vessels are in the convoy?'

'Sir, there are fifteen in total: three Panamanian, one Russian and the remainder are British.'

'Good, that's a sizeable convoy,' said Bonham-Johns. 'I want you to split the convoy in two. We need eight vessels taken out and to remain in Hvalfjörður, we'll designate that PQ7B. Instruct two Panamanian, the Russian and five British merchant vessels to remain at anchor. What escorts have been scheduled?'

'Destroyers HMS Icarus and HMS Tartar with eight armed trawlers.'

'OK, I want both destroyers held back, and half the trawlers,' added Bonham-Johns, 'PQ7A will sail as scheduled in two days.'

'But sir, that means the convoy leaving will not have sufficient armed support,' said Kinnenberg.

'Captain, the Germans have to believe that PQ7B is carrying a special cargo. That's why the escorts have to stay with that convoy. We want to tempt Tirpitz to sail and attack this apparently high-value target. We're playing the big game here.'

'Not just a big game, a dangerous game. People's lives are at stake,' said Thornton.

Bonham-Johns nodded. 'Right, now for the first round of misinformation. We need to create a false manifest for the two Panamanian-registered vessels,' he said, and handed Kinnenberg a piece of paper. 'I want that included on the manifest for both ships.'

'Norden Inc. Naval Ordnance Plant, Indianapolis, USA,' read Kinnenberg with a quizzical look.

'Do you know what they manufacture?' asked Bonham-Johns.

'No, sir,' said Kinnenberg, rather embarrassed.

'They are the makers of the most advanced and top secret tachometric bombsights, nicknamed the Blue Ox. They are compatible with the B-25J Mitchell bombers the USA are shipping to Russia.'

'The best in the world,' said Thornton with conviction.

'Yes, sir,' said Bonham-Johns, 'they are the very best, by a mile.'

'Colonel, do you really expect the Germans to fall for something that blatant?' asked Thornton.

'Sir, it's all about the way they find out. If it's from a reliable source they might fall for it. If they don't, it will take up their resources trying to determine if it is true or not.'

'It is crucial that the written manifest be filed on Sunday, in two days' time, as you normally would, no changes to procedure, nothing different,' added Bonham-Johns.

'But what is the purpose of filing it then, sir?' said Kinnenberg. 'That's the day of PQ7A's departure, and how is that information going to get to the Germans? Cargoes are strictly classified information.'

'Filed in two days as part of the manifest for convoy PQ7B, as you would normally, captain,' said Bonham-Johns.

The implication hit Kinnenberg like a thunderbolt. 'You mean?'

Bonham-Johns nodded. 'That's correct, captain. All you have to do is file it in two days, as normal, and the Germans will have it.'

Thornton stared at Bonham-Johns and swallowed so hard his Adam's apple bobbed.

'Rear Admiral, I also need to know what naval hardware you have on the east coast of the US that we might call upon for Operation Harpoon. We need to embellish the subterfuge and assemble a welcoming committee for the Führer's new toy. And, Rear Admiral, all communications on this must be sent via the US Navy Hagelin field cipher code – this is absolutely crucial, sir, the Germans need to receive this through their listening post at Noordwijk in Holland.'

Thornton looked as if he was about to burst a blood vessel.

'The President has agreed to this,' added Bonham-Johns.

Friday 19 December 1941 – 11.00 am

Porthcurno surveillance

The Stranger had been surveying the area for several hours. He'd left Fern Cottage before dawn and had checked the trip wires he'd set. They were untouched but he was troubled by the footprints he'd left in the fresh snow as he crossed the fields. It was bitterly cold in the strong north-easterly wind but the bright sunshine gave him crystal clear detail of the whole area.

He lay against a hedge high up on the west side of the Porthcurno valley with an unhindered view from the moors inland right down to the sea. He could remain out of sight from the footpath the other side of the hedge, and the field behind lay fallow so no farmer was likely to disturb him. The only problem was he could only get there and back when it was dark.

He focused his binoculars to the left at the top of the valley and at a row of granite stone terraced cottages that according to his map were named Boscarn Hamlets. That's where that annoying fat woman lives, he thought. Further up the road were three hexagonal military pillboxes, with gun barrels protruding, well camouflaged but clearly visible. These defended the northern approach to the valley.

Scanning the valley below him he counted three more pillboxes in front of a large well camouflaged brick building nestled under the eastern side of the steep valley. It had been cleverly disguised by painting the outer wall with trees and bushes. That's got to be the old telegraph station, he thought, and focused his attention on that for some time. The building was surrounded by a substantial security fence, and behind it and a little to the north he could make out a large but well camouflaged concrete structure. That must be the entrance to the underground facility, he thought.

In the field immediately above he saw a sandbagged gun emplacement covered in camouflage netting. Now, that's interesting, he thought, I wonder what that's for? Looking further down into the village there were two more pill boxes and no less than two checkpoints both guarded by similar sandbagged gun emplacements. At least twenty soldiers in total – that meant there had to be at least a hundred troops overall. This he needed to study in more detail.

Further down the road he could see a building with a big sign saying Bus Stop and thought it strange that last night the bus hadn't stopped there but further up in the village square. It must have been due to the ice and snow, he thought.

To his right, Porthcurno beach was an arc of golden sand set off by the turquoise of the ocean. Its beauty was marred by barbed wire and steel antitank 'hedgehog' bollards. Red warning signs indicated the beach was mined. On both sides of the valley there were more strategically placed pillboxes.

At Percella Point on the far side of the beach and set into the sheer cliff was a large concrete structure covered with camouflage nets clearly housing anti-aircraft guns. Below it was a large concrete bunker with a long curved front, again covered in netting. Below him on his side of the valley was Minack Point and at the foot of the cliffs were a further three pillboxes.

The authorities had clearly taken security to the highest level, he thought. Pencil and sketch pad in hand, he drew the layout of the valley and the various military installations and counted and timed the Regular Soldiers and Home Guard movements and paid particular attention to the civilians entering and leaving the security area.

He lay back in the hedge, put the pencil in his mouth and pondered. An idea started to form. Yes, he thought to himself, that's the next step, and he felt a tremor of excitement at the prospect. He looked up at the long afternoon shadows and prepared to return to Fern Cottage.

Saturday 20 December 1941 – 7.00 pm

Noordwijk, occupied Netherlands

In the Deutsche Reichspost listening station in the Dutch town of Noordwijk, Captain Klaus Wenger was in charge of a team of thirty-six operators intercepting and deciphering Allied coded transmissions.

In 1935, Wenger had joined the Lorenz Company in Berlin, the developer and manufacturer of the original Enigma cipher machine. He had been a top student at the University of Freiburg in the Faculty of Mathematics and Physics. Whilst with Lorenz he was part of the team that made successive improvements to their military Enigma machines. Being fluent in English he was loaned to the German Navy's B-Dienst surveillance service in 1938 where he was involved in developing decoding machines aimed at reading American coded communications. Their efforts developed to the point where the Deutsche Reichspost was able to break the scrambled voice transmission of the American–British transatlantic telephone system. By 1940 they were routinely listening to classified telephone conversations between Roosevelt and Churchill.

Their rate of message decryption had taken a step change increase when Germany invaded The Netherlands in May 1940 and they were able to set up a station in Noordwijk, south west of Amsterdam. Being four hundred miles closer to London than their original station in Bavaria, it gave them much stronger signals, and the amount of radio traffic and strategic information gathered had risen significantly.

Much of the messaging was mundane and boring and it was Wenger's job to identify the important transmissions. The operators handed Wenger written notes on the messages they'd overheard. 'lancelot to guinevere heading west stop disembark at skylark stop seasons compliments stop' he read. What the hell does that mean? he wondered, but it needed to be checked in case it was coded. He worked through dozens of notes, mostly wishing one another 'seasons greetings'. The Allies, for their part, had deliberately increased their radio traffic because they knew the Germans were able to decipher some of their messages. More messages meant more work for them and a higher chance that an important message would slip through unspotted.

Wenger forwarded the ones of interest to the various military Headquarters using the Enigma cipher. The majority of the messages they picked up were naval intelligence and these were forwarded to Admiral Karl Donitz's bunker in the French port of Lorient on the Atlantic coast. From there Donitz orchestrated naval strategy in the seas and oceans of northwest Europe and across the Atlantic to the east coast of the USA. He calculated his moves like a wily chess-master and changed his U-boat strategy and tactics regularly, based upon the decrypted information. With targets selected and patrol lines secured across likely convoy routes, orders went out: 'attack and report sinkings'.

Before the US had entered the war earlier that month, the Germans had deciphered most of the American naval codes including the Hagelin field cipher. This had come in very useful now that the USA had declared war and were an enemy. Wenger had noted the arrival of Rear Admiral Leonard Thornton in Reykjavik in the post of Chief of the North Atlantic Convoy Operations. Wenger enjoyed Thornton's communications. They were always to the point, bombastic and regularly used the US Naval Hagelin codes they had already broken.

On Thursday that week Thornton had communicated that Arctic Convoy PQ7 would sail tomorrow, Sunday 21st, but yesterday it was communicated that part of the convoy would be held back at Hvalfjörður Fjord. The mobilized convoy had been re-designated PQ7A and had filed their manifest and were now due to sail with minimal escort. The delayed convoy PQ7B comprised two Panamanian, one Russian and five British merchant vessels but as yet there was no departure date. The escort consisted of the destroyers HMS Icarus, HMS Tartar and four armed trawlers.

Unusually, the two Panamanian ships had arrived direct from Boston, Massachusetts. Normally the convoys were made up of ships from the east coast that sailed via Liverpool, as the others of

PQ7 had done. The convoy was scheduled to sail to Archangel, however the White Sea had frozen in mid-December and the destination had been changed to Murmansk. The B-Dienst team at Noordwijk were very interested in what the two Panamanian ships were carrying and why they had been delayed.

This announcement coincided with a visit to Hvalfjörður by Churchill's new Personal Operations Liaison Officer, Colonel Julian Bonham-Johns. They had monitored him for some time whilst he'd worked at the Special Operations Executive where he'd had responsibility for training and supplying the French resistance. Was that a coincidence, was it a routine visit or was it linked? He forwarded the information to Donitz in Lorient.

He also had a report from U-502 that the British battleship Duke of York had sailed from Scapa Flow two days before, heading north escorted by the destroyers Faulknor, Foresight and Matabele. This was clearly a significant move but for what purpose? Was this to potentially protect the PQ7B Arctic Convoy operation? If it was, the Allies were taking that convoy very seriously indeed. But then a further message this time from their Agent on the Isle of Arran reported that the Duke of York and its three escorts had reappeared anchored off Greenock in the Clyde. This in itself was puzzling and needed to be communicated. He tagged it as priority one and sent the information by Enigma code to both Donitz and Berlin.

At 9.50 pm Wenger was coming to the end of his shift and he stretched stiffly. He had a small pile of notes remaining but his head was buzzing with conflicting information and he thought, to hell with it. He had a date with a pretty young Dutch girl called Caja and, if recent progress was anything to go by, tonight might be the night. He couldn't wait.

Sunday 21 December 1941 – 4.00 am

Cabinet War Rooms, London

Colonel Julian Bonham-Johns had had a restless night sleeping in his newly assigned box room in the Cabinet War Rooms deep below Whitehall. Being Churchill's new Personal Operations Liaison Officer actually afforded him few privileges, and living like a mole underground was certainly not one of them. Whilst about as safe and secure as it was possible to be in London, it was a place of frenetic information gathering and stressful decision making. There was camaraderie amongst its occupants but it was claustrophobic and worst of all, smelly.

He awoke early to the dull throb of the fresh air supply coming through the large white-painted metal ducting in the ceiling and his mouth was as dry as a bone. He switched on the bedside table light, took a drink from the glass of water and lay there staring at the steel girders in the ceiling. In his mind he went through his day's itinerary. As a priority he had to finalise his written brief to Churchill, get it typed and presented to him in person at 9 am.

Twenty minutes later he had a flannel wash using the bowl of water on the dressing table at the end of the bed. He tried to get a lather with the soap on his badger hair shaving brush but it was difficult with cold water. Oh for some hot water and a nice bath, he thought. When he'd finished he used his aftershave liberally to try and mask the mustiness of his clothes. Everything down there smelled the same after a couple of days.

He then left his room, locked the door and walked down the maze of corridors to the toilets and then onto the small canteen for breakfast. Whilst subject to much the same rations as the general public, they were treated to regular bacon and eggs and as much tea, coffee and sugar as they wanted.

Returning to his room through the maze of corridors, he passed the kitchen and Lucy appeared.

'Oh, hello again, colonel, nice to see you,' she said and held out her hand, and again the touch lingered. He thought how beautiful, slim and shapely she was.

'I hear you've moved in with us, so you'll be suffering my tea and coffee day and night,' she added, with a barely perceptible emphasis on night. Her smile was captivating and had a vulnerability that completely disarmed him.

'Well, Lucy, I think your tea is lovely and I look forward to many—' but he stopped, realising he was making a fool of himself. Lucy gave a little mock-curtsy and went about her work.

Having prepared the briefing, Bonham-Johns waited in the office of Churchill's Principal Private Secretary for his 9 am appointment. Sir Alistair Wilson was the ultimate civil servant, dedicated, effective and well connected. He made things happen with scrupulous efficiency. His office was the only point of access into Churchill's office and he guarded it like his personal territory.

The red phone on Sir Alistair's desk rang.

'Wilson,' he said into the mouth piece, 'who shall I say is calling?' and with his hand over the mouth piece said, 'It's Brigadier Latcham for you, colonel, do you want to take it here?'

'Yes, that's fine thanks,' he said and took the phone. 'Hello, Bonham-Johns here.'

'Julian, it's Cliff. We've intercepted another coded message from Agent Banjo, it appears that our friend Stiletto has arrived, and we've got a better fix but again I'm afraid the transmission wasn't long enough to triangulate the source accurately. We've got it down to southwest Devon or southern Cornwall.'

'Well thanks, Cliff. Listen, is there any way we can further increase the number of VIs we have around Devonport? I think that's got to be the target and that would help, wouldn't it?'

'Julian, it's the length of transmission that's crucial, but yes, the more we have the higher the chance of success. Let me get onto Travis and see if we can increase the number of VIs even faster,' said Latcham.

'Good work. Keep me informed. Any news on Norway?'

'Yes, we have Agent Aurora and two others in the vicinity, and they're going to check on the recent activity we've picked up in the Fættenfjord and Beitstadfjord area northeast of Trondheim.'

'That's good, I can't emphasise how important that intelligence is. It will influence our plan of action against Tirpitz,' added Bonham-Johns.

9 am came and went and it was clear that Churchill was locked in a vigorous debate with two, possibly three people, and he was in a feisty mood. He clearly disagreed with whoever was in the room, and Bonham-Johns caught the odd snippet of conversation. Given the Prime Minister's mood he thought it wise to refresh himself on the briefing he was about to give.

Finally the door opened and Churchill's voice followed the two senior RAF officers out, a haze of cigar smoke around them.

'Over my dead body will we waste resources on such an ill-conceived plan.' The officers looked shaken and harassed.

'Alistair,' he shouted, 'more coffee.'

'Would you like one, colonel?' Sir Alistair asked.

Bonham-Johns nodded and Sir Alistair picked up one of the many black phones on his desk and said, 'Coffee for the Prime Minister and one guest,' and put the phone down.

When the green light flashed on Sir Alistair's desk, he nodded at Bonham-Johns to go through. Adjusting his uniform and brushing his hair back, he knocked and walked in.

'Good morning, Mr Churchill.'

'Hello, Julian. We'll have to be brief I'm afraid. As you know I'm leaving for the USA this afternoon and need to be out of here within the hour.'

There was a knock on the door and Lucy came in with a tray of coffee and put it on Churchill's desk. Sir Alistair was in close attendance, following right behind her.

'Are my bags ready to go, Alistair?'

'Yes, Mr Churchill,' he said.

'Good. Add this Gladstone of papers, please. I need to go through them on the flight. Let me know the moment the car arrives, oh and please have a flask of coffee ready.'

'Yes, Mr Churchill,' he said, and left closing the door.

'Well, Julian, four more war ships sunk in the Atlantic this week and a further two hundred thousand tons of merchant shipping sits on the sea bed; and that's before Tirpitz is commissioned. Word from the Far East is that Hong Kong is about to fall

51

to the Japanese and our Commonwealth troops are being pushed back in North Africa by the Germans and the Italians. Dark days, Julian, I hope you have some good news for me. How is Operation Harpoon going?'

'Sir, the latest intelligence suggests that Tirpitz is within a couple of weeks of commissioning. Leaving Wilhelmshaven, we believe she'll head up the North Sea to attack the Arctic Convoys taking shelter and replenishing in one of the Norwegian fjords. We have four operational plans in action.'

'First, we have a hoax Arctic convoy set up – PQ7B. We've let it be known that there is some highly sensitive equipment on board the convoy that the Germans will not want the Russians to get their hands on. That might entice Tirpitz out of port at a time of our choosing.'

'Second, we have conceptual agreement from the Admiralty that HMS Prince of Wales and HMS Hotspur will be released from operations in the Mediterranean to be re-positioned in the Western Approaches and make sure she doesn't escape west through the English Channel. They will have full-time air reconnaissance and air support,' said Bonham-Johns.

'My boy, that's a big ask,' Churchill replied. 'Our Naval and Merchant fleets are taking a hammering in the Mediterranean. Malta is under siege and if we lose that to the Axis forces our air cover in North Africa is lost and Rommel and his Panzer Corp will have a free ride to Cairo. Damn it, boy, we can ill afford Prince of Wales and Hotspur at such a critical time!'

'I do understand, sir, but it's vital we contain Tirpitz within the North Sea and hunt her down and destroy her, or at least disable her. Imagine her escaping west to eventually shell Gibraltar, which she could do with relative impunity. What would be the effect on our forces in the Mediterranean then? Sir, we have to get them released and only you can authorize that,' added Bonham-Johns.

Churchill stared at him expressionless. Whilst he didn't like the reallocation concept he could see that failure to do so could potentially have worse consequences.

'And third, Sir, we'll also need some additional 'big guns' in the northern North Sea because we don't have anything available. Crucially, we need to call upon US Naval ships out of the east coast but they seem reluctant to release them. I have spoken with Rear Admiral Thornton on several occasions but he has not yet come up with the goods. Quite frankly he seems a bit of an Ahab character.'

'Well, Julian the east coast of America has been harried by U-boats, and shipping has been sunk in New York harbour, if you can imagine the audacity. Our US friends are naturally very concerned about this. They are not used to being attacked on mainland America. They're still smarting from Pearl Harbour and focusing on the Pacific.'

'Sir, we have to look at the big picture. If Tirpitz escapes, the US will have a lot more to be worried about than a few sunken cargo ships. Picture her shelling Boston, New York or Long Island. Sir, we need to have the battleship USS Washington and the heavy cruisers USS Wichita and USS Tuscaloosa join us at Scapa Flow in the Orkney Islands. Even if we get them released in a week's time it will still take them six days to make the crossing and that's only just enough time.'

'My boy, Pearl Harbour has just been bombed and you want me to ask Roosevelt to focus on Hitler in Europe?'

'Yes, sir, I do,' said Bonham-Johns, holding Churchill's stare.

Churchill fiddled with his cigar and stared at it as if to get inspiration.

'Anything else, Julian?'

'Yes, sir. We have just received intelligence that the German destroyers Richard Beitzen, Paul Jakobi and Bruno Heinemann are in the Baltic Sea on exercises, and we believe they will provide support for Tirpitz when she breaks cover. We have devised a plan to attack the three using heavy bombers with a fighter escort.'

'For God's sake, Julian, you can't bomb ships in the ocean. That's bound to fail. Besides, we can't afford the bombers. They are spoken-for on priority targets for months to come.'

'Sir, we have no naval capability in that sector, so air operations are the only option. They don't have effective Flak cover out at sea and the ship's anti-aircraft capability is probably to just twelve thousand feet so the chances of success with minimum losses are high. I agree these appear low-level targets, but on the contrary I can't think of a higher priority,' said Bonham-Johns in a rather exasperated tone.

'Julian, you will not get the bombers, is that clear? It's just not going to happen. That's final.'

The silence that followed was penetrating. Bonham-Johns had not seen Churchill like this before; his left eye had developed a nervous twitch.

In a more conciliatory tone, Bonham-Johns said, 'Sir, whatever we can do to degrade their capacity to support Tirpitz, every broken link in their chain armour means a higher probability of success for Operation Harpoon.'

Churchill rubbed his eye and looked at Bonham-Johns but said nothing.

'Sir, you're going to meet with Roosevelt in five days. You have to persuade him and Admiral Wilcox to release the Washington, Wichita and Tuscaloosa then and there. We don't have any time to spare. We will release PQ7B when they are in place at Scapa Flow, which might just push the advantage our way.'

A new plume of smoke rolled up to the yellow-stained ceiling.

'Julian, you play a hard game,' said Churchill earnestly, still agitated.

There was a knock on the door.

'Mr Churchill, your car has arrived and, oh, here is your flask.'

'Thank you, Lucy,' said Sir Alistair hesitantly, sensing the tension between the two. Lucy handed over the flask, picked up the empty cups on Churchill's desk and left the room.

'Oh, sir, one last thing,' said Bonham-Johns, 'I have developed some code words for Operation Harpoon. We can't risk German intelligence getting hold of this one.'

Churchill grabbed the sheet of paper and said, 'Come with me, my boy. Let's talk some more on the way to the airport.'

Monday 22 December 1941 – 6.00 am

Noordwijk, occupied Netherlands

Wenger was feeling very happy with himself. Saturday night had indeed turned out much as he'd hoped, and the gorgeous Caja had started to succumb to his attentions. He was planning ahead for Christmas Eve and needed to get a hotel room or at least somewhere warm. It was perishing cold in a Noordwijk alleyway on a December night. But it had been worth it. God, she is so gorgeous, he thought.

He stared at the pile of messages that had built up on his desk. 'OK, team,' he shouted, 'anything I need to know about?'

'Captain, the Duke of York is on the move and there's some chatter to and from Norway towards the top of the priority pile,' said Stefan Merensky, his lead operator.

Wenger worked through the pile and found the three messages. According to their agent on the Isle of Arran, the Duke of York and her three escorts had set sail at 6 pm yesterday evening heading due west. Now I wonder where they're going, he thought as he notified Donitz.

The other message was intriguing and clearly important. The decoded message was from MI5 to an Agent Aurora that read, 'check activity in fjords stop priority for harpoon stop report immediately stop'. So what's this harpoon, he wondered, is this a new weapon, a mini submarine? It clearly had something to do with checking new developments in the fjords, but what and where? The return message simply said, 'confirm stop'. Whoever sent that clearly didn't want to be located.

'Stefan, where do we have listening posts in Norway?'

'Just a minute, captain, I'll get the list.'

Wenger checked through the other messages in the pile.

'Here it is,' said Merensky, 'there's not many, actually. We have three in Oslo, one in each of Kristiansand, Stavanger, Bergen and Narvik and four in Trondheim.'

That makes sense, Wenger thought, Trondheim is a strategic port for attacking North Atlantic and Arctic convoys. Why would

MI5 be interested in any of the other cities? From a military perspective it had to be Trondheim, surely? Wenger sent an urgent coded message to German military headquarters in Oslo.

Tuesday 23 December 1941 – 5.00 pm
Nanjizal Head, Cornwall

Bert Chenoweth got up earlier than normal and by the time he left Boscarn Hamlets light was fading fast in the western sky. He walked quickly to the village hall and met with the other Home Guard soldiers for their orders.

'Evening, men. Now, listen up,' said Captain Tregoning addressing the soldiers. He had been discharged from the army when he was wounded in the First World War and enjoyed the thrill of being back in the military.

'We have reports of some strange goings-on up around Boswednack Farm. A man or men have been sighted although it's probably a poacher, but Harry emphatically denies it.'

There was a general chuckle. They all knew Harry Nancarrow, indeed nearly every one of them had had pigeon, rabbits or a cut of venison from him. Many had got their meat for the Christmas table from him.

'You never know who's out there,' said Tregoning, 'so I want you in pairs, Josh and Pete, you patrol the path from Nanjizal Bay up to Kenidjack Farm. Bert and Will you work between Boswednack Farm and St Levan. Ernie and Walter, you patrol south towards Carn Glaze Farm. Remember, if you're in trouble, two shots in the air and wait for support. Off you go.'

All six checked their ammunition and left together for the steep walk out of the valley and up towards Polgassick. The evening was cold and clear with a near-full moon rising in the east. At Tall Cross junction the three pairs split and quietly and cautiously went to their assigned areas.

Bert and Will Tarraway walked up the track towards Boswednack Farm and then detoured through a gate and across a field. They had a favoured spot where they had a good view of the farm and surrounding area. They dropped down out of sight and shared a thermos flask of hot tea. They had been friends for nearly thirty years, since they'd both enlisted in the Duke of Cornwall's Light Infantry in 1915. They had seen front-line action on the Somme and both had been wounded more than once. Their rural guile had made them ideal members of the elite 'A' Company trench-raiding parties of the 6th Service Battalion. There was still chemistry between them; they worked well together and instinctively covered one another's back.

'Let's try and find Harry Nancarrow. He'll know better than anyone what's going on,' said Bert. They scanned the area in silence.

'Hey Bert,' whispered Will, 'look over here.'

Bert peered over the wall. 'What is it?' he whispered.

'Twenty yards right of the gate and just to the left of the tree, I'm sure there's a figure tucked in close to the hedge moving left to right, towards the farm.'

'I don't see nothing,' said Bert. 'Who do you reckon it is?'

Will looked again. 'Bugger,' he said, 'I can't see nothing now, whoever it was he don't want to be seen.'

'Alright, let's go and investigate. Better fix bayonets,' said Bert.

They made their way to the hedge where Will had thought he'd seen the man. Bert briefly shone his torch on the ground and fresh footprints in the frozen snow were clear to see.

'OK, let's go,' said Bert.

They followed the footsteps along the hedge but lost them on a rocky track.

'Shit,' whispered Will, 'typical.'

They waited and listened intently. They could hear a faint rustling in the hedge ahead ... was it a rabbit? Then to their right a cracking of twigs and something much larger than a rabbit started to move.

Bert raised his rifle in a flash and shouted, 'Halt or I'll shoot.'

Then behind them there was a voice.

Alarmed, Bert swung his rifle around and was about to shoot but heard the words just in time.

'Don't shoot, it's me, Harry!'

'Jesus Christ Harry you bloody fool. Come out where we can see you,' hissed Bert, his heart thumping in his ears. The movement on the right reappeared, barking and snarling.

'Harry, that bloody dog will be the death of you,' said Bert. 'One day a trigger-happy soldier is going to shoot you both.'

'Sorry, Bert. I know he's daft's a brush but he's a rare hunter.'

'Bloody liability if you ask me,' added Will.

'Listen, shut that bloody dog up and tell me have you seen anything suspicious out here in the last few nights, or is it you spooking our soldiers?'

'Not me, Bert, they don't see me, they're night-blind.'

'Well, have you seen anything?' repeated Will.

'Yes, like I said to Cap'n Tregoning there's been a bloke around Boswednack Farm.'

'Who is it?' prompted Will.

'Dunno, not from around here,' Harry replied.

'Is he out tonight?' asked Bert.

'Haven't seen him. I've been setting snares down in bottom field.'

'Alright, Harry, if you see anyone strange out here, anyone at all, let me know as quickly as you can,' added Bert, 'and keep that bloody dog under control or you'll both be history.'

Harry tied some cord around the dog's neck and led him off down the track.

'Will, let's go and check the farm, although anyone within a hundred miles will have heard that commotion,' said Bert.

They moved off west, keeping to the dark side of the hedge, crunching through the icy snow. When they got to the yard at the back of Boswednack Farm they waited quietly out of sight beside the barn. They could hear the sounds of the night, a fox yelping in the distance and an owl hooting nearby. They waited for what seemed an age but heard nothing suspicious; the house was in darkness.

'No one about. Do you reckon he could be in the house?' whispered Bert.

'Could be. Why the hell would he come this way if he wasn't visiting, and why would he be visiting Eleanor so secretively?' queried Will.

'Your guess is as good as mine,' whispered Bert, 'her husband has been dead for near, what, six years must be, perhaps, well you know? Anyway best be on our guard, you never know what might be going on so close to the Telegraph. I'll go over by the well... you stay here.'

After a further fifteen minutes Bert was starting to lose interest when the latch on the back door of the farmhouse gave a click and the door opened and two figures appeared out of the darkness.

Bert stood up and with his torch and rifle pointed at the pair.

'Don't move. Home Guard.'

The Stranger's right hand dived into his coat pocket.

'Keep your hands where I can see them,' said Bert sensing immediate danger. The two stood still as ordered and Will appeared from beside the barn.

'Evening, Mrs Bannencourt,' said Will from the shadows to her left.

She nearly fainted with surprise and the Stranger was about to run but thought better of it.

'Oh, evening, Will,' she said barely able to speak. 'You gave me such a start.'

'Sorry,' he said, 'just a routine patrol. Who might you be?' asked Will, shining his torch in the man's face. He wore a black Fedora hat and a long black coat with the hat partially covering a bandaged wound on his forehead.

'Oh, he's a friend of my late husband, he's just visiting,' she said, her voice still wavering.

'So why didn't you use the track then, Mr ... uh?'

'Lavine,' he said, 'Rod Lavine.'

'So Mr Lavine, why not walk along the farm track like everyone one else?'

The Stranger hesitated, his mind a complete blank. 'Uh well truth be told, I didn't want to be seen, if you know what I mean. A stranger calling on a widow, you know.'

Even in the weak moonlight it was clear Eleanor Bannencourt was uncomfortable.

'Just a friend,' she blurted.

'So everything is alright then?' queried Bert.

'Yes, everything is fine,' she added. She wanted to say, 'I'd rather you didn't mention this,' but she thought better of it.

The Stranger turned and kissed her on the cheek and said, 'Merry Christmas, Elly, see you again.'

'Goodbye, Rod, good to see you.'

'So where is it you're staying?' asked Bert.

'St Levan,' said the Stranger and he turned to go.

'Where in St Levan?' asked Bert in an icy, impatient tone. The Stranger was livid for letting himself get so easily cornered, but he had no option.

'Fern Cottage, just down from the church.'

'Who owns Fern Cottage?' demanded Bert.

'Oh I can't remember, I've got it written down somewhere,' and he put his hand into the right pocket of his coat.

'I've rented it from Betty George,' blurted Eleanor Bannencourt. 'She's staying with her daughter Elaine in Penzance for Christmas.' The tension eased. Well that makes sense, thought Bert. He knew it was Betty's cottage.

'Right, I'll be off then,' said the Stranger, and with that he disappeared across the yard and down the track.

'You sure you're alright, Mrs Bannencourt?' asked Will.

'Quite sure,' she said.

'You can't be too careful,' added Will, 'he's not from around here is he? What did he say his name was?'

Her mind froze in panic for a split second but then it came back to her.

'Roden, I mean, Rodney Lavine,' she stuttered, 'good night,' and went back in the house, closed the door and hurriedly slid the bolt.

'Well what do you make of that, Bert?' asked Will.

'Something's not quite as it seems, that's for sure. They obviously know one another, and she has been a widow all that time. By all accounts, her husband died when they lived overseas, and she moved over here.'

'Well I suppose after all those years—' but Will left the remainder unsaid.

'Mmm I'm not so sure,' said Bert, 'let's have a look around. I have a strange feeling about this.'

They checked the outhouses and the old stable, all now disused.

'I'll just check the barn,' said Bert, and after a couple of minutes returned.

'Nothing,' he said, 'let's go back and report, but I think a detour to Fern Cottage would not go amiss.'

As they walked down the track towards St Levan, two sets of eyes watched their every step. The Stranger, hiding by the hedge, and Eleanor Bannencourt, looking through the kitchen window. When they had disappeared from sight the Stranger retraced his steps back to Boswednack Farm.

There needed to be a change of plan.

Tuesday 23 December 1941 – 8.00 pm
Noordwijk, occupied Netherlands

A transmission from Agent Violin was reporting a new British initiative called Operation Harpoon. This was reliably attributed to Churchill and his direct aids so had to be of strategic importance. All that was known was that it was a naval initiative, and there were code words associated with it so was likely to be North Atlantic or Mediterranean focused. Aha, thought Wenger, harpoon comes up again, and it's Operation Harpoon and it involves Norway so we can rule out the Mediterranean. They needed to know more detail and put out a message to all their Agents to listen for any potential chatter.

Violin also reported that Churchill had flown to the USA on the 21st December.

'Damn it, he'll already be there. What a missed opportunity,' Wenger said out loud. 'Why the hell do we get such priceless information two days late?'

He forwarded it to Berlin secure in the knowledge that Agent Violin was going to get a fire cracker up his backside for the late report.

'Has anyone received an update on the Duke of York and her escort?' he asked.

'Nothing, captain, but there is something in from Osmar,' replied Merensky.

The message from Agent Osmar in Norfolk, Virginia reported increased activity in and around Chesapeake Bay. Norfolk was the biggest US Navy base on the east coast of the United States, and the Germans had two agents based there. Osmar reported increased anti-submarine activity with two Fletcher class destroyers, USS Nicholas and USS O'Bannon, patrolling the entrance to Chesapeake Bay. Was that important he wondered.

Wenger stretched and rubbed his face. Oh, he was looking forward to having a drink with Caja tomorrow night. She had organised a room for them to spend the night at her friend's house just around the corner from the pub. The friend had gone to stay with her parents for Christmas.

'It's only a single bed but it's so warm and cosy,' Caja had said.

He imagined the delectable pleasures of spending the night being squeezed against Caja's naked body.

Wednesday 24 December 1941 – 2.00 pm
Fættenfjord, Norway

Axel Hansen was in trouble. Overhead he was being hunted by a single-engine Fieseler Storch spotter plane and in the valley below him he could clearly hear a platoon of German troops methodically working their way up the gorge toward him. The spotter plane was a particular problem as it had him pinned down amongst trees. His next move had to be across open ground and he'd be a sitting duck. He was tempted to shoot at the plane; it was so low and slow it would be an easy target, but the shot would give away his position. Taking stock of the situation he realised he'd be captured or worse if he didn't do something very quickly.

Peering cautiously over the rocks, he saw the Germans slowly but surely closing on his position. Removing his gloves he pulled three hand grenades from his backpack and lined them up on the snow-covered boulder in front of him. The plane was making the final turn for another approach and when it was lined up on his position he grabbed the grenades one at a time, pulled the pin, and lobbed them into the gorge below him. Before the first one had exploded he had his rifle in hand and, resting on the rock, aimed at the slowly approaching plane. The three hand grenades exploded in sequence and there were shouts and screams. Bullets started zinging off the rocks around him. Oblivious to the flying rock fragments, he aimed and managed to fire four shots at the plane. He wasn't happy with the first, doubted the second but was confident of the last two as the plane zoomed overhead and disappeared from sight. He was sure he'd hit it but there was no telltale smoke or change in pitch of the engine.

Taking three more grenades from his backpack, he glanced down the gorge looking for the troopers, and to his relief they appeared to have retreated, at least temporarily. Lobbing the grenades as far as he could he listened to them clatter down the rock face towards the position where he guessed the troopers were regrouping. The explosions were accompanied by further screams and figures running helter-skelter down the gorge. That would give him a good fifteen minute head start, he thought, and quickly made his way to the edge of the trees. He scanned the sky and listened but heard no plane. With that, he broke out his skis and set off in a northerly direction at a fast pace.

The sun had dropped behind the mountain to his left and he was glad to be in the deepening shade that moved across the vast snow-covered plateau. After nearly thirty minutes of hard uphill skiing he dropped behind a rock to catch his breath. Pulling out his binoculars, he scanned the route he'd taken and was concerned at how obvious the ski tracks were. In the far distance he could make out black specks, maybe five or six soldiers following him, at least fifteen to twenty minutes behind him. He scanned the darkening sky but to his relief he couldn't see or hear a plane. From the air he'd be located in seconds.

The wind was picking up and a bank of purple cloud to the east caught the last reflections of the setting sun. Minutes later, the wind started to swirl and blow snow grains in sheets across the icy surface. He started to feel more relaxed; he now had the advantage; he was on home turf and the weather was on his side. He'd been hunting in these mountains in all weathers from the day he could walk. He put his head down and broke into a running action with parallel skis, kicking and gliding with each stride, the poles planted alternately on the opposite side to the kick. He could keep this up for hours if necessary.

After more than an hour of punishing skiing and in steady driving snow, he reached the rendezvous, a small wooden hut set low under a river bank in thick woodland. He took off his skies and back pack and rifle. There was no light showing from the hut but he detected the faint smell of woodsmoke and cooking food. He approached the hut and pulled the hidden lever under a lean-to. Inside the hut, the oil light hanging from the roof swayed in response. Moments later the lever clicked back in place, confirming acknowledgement from within the hut.

Grabbing his gear, Hansen opened the hut door and went into the small vestibule. With the outer door closed and bolted he knocked the agreed code on the inner door and entered. Two heavily bearded men sat on the benches either side of the central table. Both had a rifle pointing straight at him. To his left was the older of the two, Kristian Malmvig, with his craggy tanned face resembling strips of air-dried reindeer meat. The young man opposite him, Arvid Karlsen, was in his thirties and had a bright red sheen on his round cheeks. He'd clearly only just got back from being out in the bitter cold.

'So?' enquired Malmvig, keeping his rifle pointed. 'You are late. Is all good?' Hansen nodded.

'Are you sure?' Malmvig asked again.

'Ya,' said Hansen nodding his head in the agreed manner, 'ya, I was pinned down at the Struka Gorge for some time but I escaped and lost them on the plateau over an hour ago.'

'Coffee?' asked Karlsen.

'Ya please, Arvid, with a good slug of akvavit. It's bloody cold out there.'

'Tell me,' said the old man, finally lowering his rifle, 'did you find anything?'

'Ya I did,' said Hansen, 'I was there six or seven months ago and there was only the old fish drying factory, and now that is gone and the Germans are building something new. It's a hive of activity.'

He pulled out a map and unfolded it on the table.

'They're here in this bay on the east side of Fættenfjord. I went down through the gorge and kept to the trees well above the road running along the fjord. There's regular military and construction traffic and foot patrols as well. From this bluff I got a pretty good view of the site, and they have constructed three large tanks here and there are four smaller ones along this side.' He pointed with his fat stubby forefinger. 'The big tanks are easily one hundred feet in diameter.'

'On the edge of this rock outcrop they have a berth where small freighters tie up and deliver fuel to the tanks. There was one offloading this morning.'

'Those are huge tanks,' said Malmvig, 'they could probably hold close to maybe ten thousand tons of bunker fuel each?'

'Ya, I would say so, and what's even more interesting,' said

Hansen, 'is that on the edge of the fjord they're constructing six huge bollards. It's clear they are expecting a very large visitor'.

'That is good work, Axel, and you got back safely. That is also good,' said Malmvig with a smile.

'Mmm, only just, it was one of those foot patrols that picked up my tracks in the forest. I have to say it was touch and go for a while. And one thing's for sure: the Germans will know there little secret has been blown.'

'That is true, but that will occupy their minds and make them even more fearful. That is a bonus,' he smiled. 'And tell us – how did you get on Arvid?'

Unfolding his map on the table, Karlsen took a large slug of akvavit.

'I worked around this side of Beitstadfjord, and there's a lot of activity along this shore. I couldn't get too close because I'd have had to cross this wide road and I didn't want to risk that – there's regular military patrols and a lot of traffic. With binoculars I could see large tanks being constructed. It certainly looks like a refuelling facility but it's a few weeks from being complete. What I don't understand is why they'd build two similar facilities just twenty miles apart.'

'Well, if they are the same it has to be for something important. What size are the tanks?' asked Malmvig.

'Oh, much the same as the ones Axel saw. The large tanks could easily be one hundred feet in diameter, and the anti-aircraft facilities appear to be mobile ones.'

'So, there's not much between the sites except that construction at Fættenfjord is more advanced,' said Malmvig. 'What about the air defences, Axel?'

'It's bristling with Flak anti-aircraft batteries, although they didn't appear to be manned.'

'Well, that's a good day's work. You must be hungry,' said Malmvig.

Lifting the cast iron pot from the stove he dished out three bowls of stew and they all ate enthusiastically.

'You do realise it's Christmas Eve?' offered Karlsen. 'Let's finish the akvavit and forget this lousy war for a couple of hours.'

'Remember, we need to code this information and transmit to London. We have a slot in thirty minutes, so let's get ready,' said the old man, 'but after that there's enough time to celebrate a good day's work,' he added with a wide grin.

Wednesday 24 December 1941 – 5.00 pm
Porthcurno, Cornwall

Josh Tregembo was coming to the end of his twelve hour shift. He and his team had encoded and transmitted nearly sixty-five thousand words an hour during that time. Most of the top secret messages had been destined for the USA and Canada but some had gone as far afield as Singapore and Australia. The outgoing messages originated from London via Morse code telegraph, telephone messages and a top secret bag from London that was flown into RAF Sennen five miles away, sometimes twice a day. There was another team that handled incoming messages.

One of Josh's many functions was to prioritise the messages to the busiest destinations. This involved storing lower priority messages until a line became available. Today, as was the case most days, the USA was the busiest. The messages transferred through the deep sea cables stretching between Porthcurno and Green Hill, Rhode Island, were then sent on to their final destinations usually via Washington DC by telegraph or telephone lines.

It was down to the six-man team under Josh to use the indicated cipher and code reference on each of the top secret messages. After coding, the messages were passed to the Transmission Team who typed the words onto punched paper tape using a keyboard perforator. This in turn was fed into the automatic transmitter, which would read the code and send a series of electrical pulses down the designated deep sea cable. There were fourteen cables running from Porthcurno, each to a specific destination around the world; three had been discontinued because of enemy occupation at the terminus.

Josh, being single, was scheduled to work through Christmas and due to have time off a couple of weeks later. Tonight, though, he was going to have a few drinks in the pub with a very cute land girl from Polgassick Farm who he'd met a few weeks back.

At 5.30 pm the next shift arrived. There was always a 'warm-handshake' shift change that ensured the best possible continuity in the messaging. Josh and his six team members headed to security door B for the tedious but essential 'exit door locked' process. This ensured that in case of a bombing raid the critical instrument room was always secure. The telegraphers joked that next to Churchill's Cabinet War Rooms in London they were the best protected people in the land.

Having passed through the two doors and the outer electric fence, Josh bid Merry Christmas to his colleagues and headed to the Cable Station Inn to meet Nancy. If his recent dreams were any indication, he was hoping it was going to be his best-ever Christmas.

On entering the pub, a wall of tobacco smoke and a cacophony of chatter greeted him. Despite the deprivations and worries of the war, everyone seemed intent on having a good time tonight. He looked around the packed bar but saw no sign of his girl-friend.

'Rusty,' yelled a voice further down the bar, 'what you havin'?'

'Oh, hi Rob. Half of bitter please, mate,' he replied.

A few minutes later Robert Chenoweth escaped the crush at the bar with two beers and handed one to Josh.

'Thanks, mate, much appreciated. Merry Christmas.'

'And you,' smiled Robert, and they chinked glasses.

'You haven't seen Nancy, have you?'

'No not so far. She's probably still milking at this time, isn't she?' Robert suggested. 'Look, there's a table free over there by the window. Let's sit down.'

'She said she'd be able to get away early as I've got to be on shift at four tomorrow morning.'

'Been there, done that,' sympathised Robert. 'Hey, you'll never guess what. I got a letter from the old man today via the Telegraph international bag. They've moved him from Hong Kong to Colombo, where he's heading up the Telegraph for the whole of the Indian Ocean area.'

'Wow, that's fantastic news. That's the biggest region after North America, isn't it?' he queried.

'Certainly is. Fancy another one?' asked Robert.

'No thanks, but let me get you one. Same again?' and Josh disappeared into the scrum around the bar.

71

As he returned to the table he looked around again for Nancy, but she was nowhere to be seen. Rather disheartened, he looked at his watch.

'Well I'll give her a few more minutes,' he said.

'She'll be along just now, you know what old farmer Penhallow is like, miserable old so-and-so,' comforted Robert.

'You know, I also heard today that the Telegraph Company is going to send one free telegram a month to and from children evacuated abroad. Isn't that a nice touch?' said Robert, rather proud of the esteem that it added to his company.

But Josh was distracted and not paying attention.

Again, he looked at his watch and said, 'Well thanks for the beer, Rob. Look, I'm going up to Polgassick Farm to see what's happened to Nancy.'

'OK, Josh. Have a Merry Christmas and say hi to Nancy from me and Megan,' said Robert.

'Will do,' said Josh and he exited the pub into the cold, crisp evening air.

Thursday 25 December 1941 – 7.00 am

Boscarn Hamlets, Cornwall

Clara was up early, stoking the stove in the kitchen in preparation for cooking a slap-up Christmas lunch for her family. She had decided that given the austerity that gripped the country she would go all out to make the day as jolly as she could.

She set a wood fire in the tiny dining room and rearranged her home-made Christmas decorations of holly, garden greenery and whitewashed pinecones. She had dipped the holly in Epsom salts that made it appear beautifully frosted. In the middle of the table was a colourful bowl of bright orange carrots, crimson beetroot and sprigs of green parsley. Paper chains made out of old magazines were hanging across the ceiling and a small, beautifully decorated fir tree stood in the corner.

Back in the kitchen Clara put the kettle on and started frying up rabbit kidneys, livers and onions for one of her 'winter treats' to finish off breakfast.

'Oh, Merry Christmas my love,' Clara said as Robert walked in. 'How's little May?'

'She's a bit grizzly.'

'Oh, I heard the poor little mite, come and have a cupper my love and take one through to Megan. I'll take one to Bert. He got in late again this morning. Poor old bugger, his cough is some bad,' said Clara.

There was a knock on the front door.

'I'll get it,' said Robert.

He opened the door and a young officer introduced himself, 'Captain Harvey, Duke of Cornwall Light Infantry. Can I have a word with Mr Robert Chenoweth?'

'Uh, yes of course. That's me.'

The captain looked around as if to check no one was listening.

'Oh,' said Robert, 'come in,' and led him into the dining room and closed the door. Clara heard the door shut and went to investigate, putting her ear to the door.

'Merry Christmas, Clara,' said Bert coming down the stairs, and he gave her a big hug.

'Merry Christmas, Bert,' she said. 'You can't have had more than forty winks' sleep. Come into the kitchen and have a cuppa.'

'Well I'm off tonight so I'll have a good sleep then. Who's that calling?'

'Dunno, Captain somebody-or-other. I didn't quite catch it.'

'That's not like you, Clara,' he said with a broad grin.

'Now, don't you start, Bert Chenoweth, or I'll put you on rations,' she giggled. ''Ere, sit yourself down. I'll make you a nice cuppa. Got some leaves from my Rhoda at the Star when I was in Penzance last Saturday. Makes all the difference, don't it?'

He let out a big sigh as he settled in the chair next to the stove.

'Still some snow in the shady parts,' he said. 'I can't remember the last time we had snow on the ground at Christmas. Must have been when I was a nipper. Mind, we had a terrible snow in 1917 in France. Even the mud in the trenches froze solid – and your mug of tea if you didn't drink it quickly.'

'Must have been terrible,' said Clara. 'Never mind, that's all in the past,' she said, rather hesitantly.

''Ere, get your gnashers around that, something to keep you going.' She handed him a slice of toast with a thick coating of damson jam.

'We're not going to starve this Christmas. We're going to have a lovely time,' she said.

The thought of her husband Ross all those miles away suddenly hit her. If only he were here, she thought to herself. Bert caught the moment.

'You make the best damson jam, it's delicious.'

'Well let's hope we can get preserving sugar next year,' she said. 'It's already rationed and I didn't get as much as I wanted. Still, I managed some blackberry jam as well, and that should last through to summer. We've got the chickens and the pickled veg as well, plus the rabbits you shoot. We'll be fine.'

Megan joined Clara and Bert in the kitchen with baby May.

'Merry Christmas, my love,' said Clara giving Megan a big kiss on the cheek.

'And who's having their very first Christmas?' she said to the baby, tickling her under the chin.

'Where's Robert?' asked Megan.

'Oh he's got someone come to see him, a Captain somebody, I dunno what's keeping him,' said Clara. 'This winter treat will spoil if we keep it warm any longer.'

Clara placed a spoonful of the savoury mix on the toast and topped it with a fried egg.

'Ooh, Mum, that smells fantastic,' said Megan, 'thanks so much.'

'You're most welcome,' said Clara. 'We're going to have a day when we forget the war and enjoy Christmas like we always used to.'

Megan, Bert and Clara tucked into their savoury breakfast with relish.

There were voices in the hall, then the front door banged shut and Robert walked into the kitchen.

'Everything alright, love?' asked Megan.

'Uh, yes OK,' said Robert, but it was obvious to everyone that it wasn't.

'Ere you go,' said Clara, handing him his plate of winter treat. 'That'll set you up proper. Let's all go through to the dining room and open our presents. Bring your plate with you, Robert.'

She moved the chairs to face the fire and the colourful line of stockings full of presents laid neatly either side. Despite rationing and general shortages she had prepared a very homely Christmas. She felt like a mother hen with her brood. She proudly handed each stocking to its owner, and the tiny one for May went to her mum.

'Bless us all,' said Clara, and they started to carefully unwrap their presents. A thick, woollen hand knitted jumper for Bert, a National Savings Certificate for Robert, scented soap and silk stockings for Megan, a little pink cardigan for May and some fancy candles and chocolates for Clara. There was one present left and Clara put it thoughtfully on the dresser.

'Well, didn't Father Christmas do us proud,' she said. 'We'll all share these chocolates after lunch.'

Clara collected the wrapping paper and smoothed it out, folded it neatly and wound up the string. Without a word they all knew they'd see it again next Christmas.

'Oh, I nearly forgot this,' said Robert, handing her a letter. 'It came in the Telegraph bag.'

'Oh lovely, it's from Ross,' she said and sniffed the envelope for his scent.

She opened it quickly and read it through and then gasped, 'Oh he's been transferred from Hong Kong to Colombo and he's got business in London and a five day pass at the end of January.'

Everyone cheered at the news and tears filled Clara's eyes and rolled down her cheeks.

'I do miss the old bugger,' she said.

'Enough of the old bugger, thank you, that's my son you're talking about, what does that make me?' joked Bert.

They all laughed except Robert who was still deep in thought.

Clara turned on the radio for the Home Service nine o'clock news. The King and Queen were spending Christmas at Sandringham, and there was optimism that Hitler could be defeated now that the United States had joined the war, but on a salutary note Hong Kong had surrendered to the advancing Japanese.

'Oh thank God Ross is out of there,' Clara said, putting her hands to her cheeks, her face drained of colour. 'I didn't even know Hong Kong was in danger. I hope Colombo is better?' she added.

'It is,' said Bert. 'It's quite safe there, and Ross will be fine.'

After the news, a programme of popular carols had everybody singing along whilst Clara plied them with mince pies and Christmas biscuits.

Robert became more distracted through the morning, and it finally got the better of him.

'Sorry, I've got to go down to the Telegraph for a while.'

'Oh Robert, I thought you had the day off, it's Christmas,' said Megan,

'I know, I'm sorry,' he said, 'but I've got to go down. Something's come up.'

'Make sure you're back for lunch,' Clara shouted after him, 'two o'clock sharp.'

Bert followed him out of the dining room to the front door.

'What's up, lad?' he asked.

Robert was about to speak but stopped himself. He nodded to Bert to follow him outside.

'It's, Josh Tregembo,' said Robert. 'He didn't report for work this morning and there's no sign of him at home up St Levan. And his girlfriend Nancy hasn't seen him.'

'Probably got drunk and stayed with a friend?' said Bert.

'Maybe, Granddad, but I doubt it. He was alright when he left the pub last night, he'd only had a half of beer.'

Thursday 25 December 1941 – 6.30 am
Noordwijk, occupied Netherlands

Wenger was feeling tired and more than a little hung-over. The previous night he and Caja had been drinking in De Oude Molen Inn, sitting by a roaring log fire and enjoying one another's company. They had talked about their plans over the next week or two, and Caja said she had to go and see her parents tomorrow in the nearby town of Hoofddorp and would be gone a few days. But they had all night to themselves, and they kissed and cuddled in the heat of the fire and under the haze of alcohol.

At about 10 pm he had started to feel dizzy and sick, and Caja said they should go back to her friend's flat. The frigid air helped to clear his head but as she helped him down the street he knew he was going to be ill. As he leant against the wall a military car pulled up.

'Are you alright, soldier?' the uniformed passenger said.

He tried to salute, but failed.

'Wenger, is that you, you drunken fool? What the hell are you playing at? Get in the back and leave that whore alone.'

Caja retreated into the shadows. Wenger dropped to his knees and threw up violently in the gutter. The passenger swore at him, got out, grabbed him and roughly bundled him into the back of the car.

That's all he could remember apart from being woken up that morning with a blinding headache. Four cups of coffee and three painkillers later, he was at his desk. He had the constitution of an ox. He wondered what had happened to Caja. He was frustrated that he hadn't managed to spend the night with her.

He worked slowly through the messages on his desk. He was reading reports that the destroyers Faulknor, Foresight and Matabele had been sighted at Ponta Delgada in the Azores and were being refuelled, but no sign of the Duke of York. Destroyers Highlander, Harvester and Lightning had sailed from the same port twelve hours before. Wenger smelled a rat. The Duke of York had not been seen, and that had to mean she had remained offshore and the three were taking over escort duties. But what the hell were they up to? The Azores was a refuelling point for ships bound for Southern Africa and South America, but it made no sense for such strategic vessels to be heading for either.

He sat and pondered and then realised, surely it had to be, Churchill had not been heard of for four days, yes of course. He yelled out to his team.

'The old bulldog is on board Duke of York and that's how he's getting to the USA. He didn't fly. The intelligence from Violin was wrong. The Duke of York had twice the distance capability of the destroyers. Yes, that's it. That explains the increased destroyer patrols off of Chesapeake Bay as well.'

If they had any U-boats positioned in the area they could go after Churchill. Wenger immediately sent Enigma ciphered messages to Donitz in Lorient, Agent Omar in Norfolk, Virginia, and to Berlin.

The team had also intercepted and decoded a message sent last night from Agent Aurora. It read, 'one complete stop two near complete stop detail to follow stop'.

Mmm, I wonder what that refers to, pondered Wenger. Trondheim must have picked that up if we did, he thought, and he put the message in the 'to be filed' box.

At the end of the shift he wrote a note to Caja apologising for his behaviour and hoped she'd had a good Christmas with her parents and asked if they could meet again on New Year's Eve. He was going to drop the note in at De Oude Molen but he was not stopping for a drink this time. He still didn't feel well.

Friday 26 December 1941 – 3.00 pm

Cabinet War Rooms, London

Colonel Julian Bonham-Johns was reviewing the latest intelligence information for Operation Harpoon. He had a scheduled telephone call to brief Churchill in Washington DC and needed to be up to speed.

Battleships Prince of Wales and Hotspur were due to leave the Mediterranean for the Western Approaches in the next twenty four hours. They would pass the Straits of Gibraltar at night, hugging the North African coast to minimise the chance of being seen by German spies in Spain. There had thus far been no communication from Rear Admiral Thornton on providing the three US battleships.

Thirty minutes before the call, Bonham-Johns walked down the corridor to Sir Alistair Wilson's office where he'd arranged to pick up the key. He then walked to room 63, that from the outside appeared to be a toilet, and most of the staff thought it was Churchill's personal privy. It had a lavatory stile lock that always read 'Engaged'. Inside was the Transatlantic Telephone Room with a hotline to the White House in Washington DC. Despite the subterfuge, the hotline was known to be monitored by the Germans.

He picked up the telephone receiver and dialled the number. An American voice answered, and Bonham-Johns gave the password and code and was connected to the US White House. The number rang three times and was answered by an operator.

Bonham-Johns gave a further code and the voice said, 'Please hold I'm transferring you.'

Seconds later, the line clicked and there was a gruff 'Hello, is that you, my boy?'

'Yes, sir, it is.'

'What's the status, my boy? And by the way we cannot guarantee the security of this line.'

'Pequod and Rachel escort arrival confirmed for replenishment. No word from Ahab,' said Bonham-Johns, 'any word from Bildad?'

'Yes, I can confirm Peleg and Bildad held discussions, and Queequeg and Tashtego depart tomorrow for hunting ground.'

Bonham-Johns breathed a big sigh of relief that the US had despatched two warships, but what had happened to the third?

'I look forward to meeting Queequeg and Tashtego but please confirm Daggoo to follow?' he replied.

'Negative, my boy, Daggoo not available. Peleg will meet Ahab to discuss. I need you to meet Peleg, Ahab, Starbuck and Stubb in port on the fifth. Secure orders to follow this call. Over and out.'

Well the old dog, thought Bonham-Johns, good for you. It was too bad that USS Tuscaloosa was not going to join the show, but two out of three wasn't bad given the pressures the US Navy was under.

He left the secure communications room and walked back to his office three doors down from Churchill's. Lucy was in the corridor and greeted Bonham-Johns with her usual warm smile.

'Can I bring you a cup of tea, and a piece of Christmas cake? No icing, I'm afraid.'

'That would be lovely, thank you, Lucy,' he said.

Five minutes later, she appeared with a silver service tray that was normally used to serve Churchill.

'Don't tell The Boss,' she whispered conspiratorially and with a smile that went straight to his heart. Her slim, shapely body was the fantasy of his most intimate dreams. He was lost for words for a few seconds.

'Yes, thank you, Lucy. That's our secret.'

She sat on his bed and asked, 'Did you manage to speak with The Boss, and is he in good spirits?'

'Yes a little tired, I guess, but OK,' said Bonham-Johns before he thought of the sensitivity of the question.

'It is quiet without him, isn't it?' she added. 'We all feel at sixes and sevens when he's not here.' She continued, 'I hope he'll be back soon?'

'Nothing will keep him away for long. He loves your coffee so much,' said Bonham-Johns with a smile, thinking the question a little brazen.

'Oh now, that's just taking the Mick,' said Lucy. 'Can I pour you another tea?'

'Uh, yes that would be, lovely, uh nice, thanks,' said Bonham-Johns, getting tongue tied.

'Julian, if you don't mind me calling you that, a couple of us are going for a drink at The Red Lion at Derby Gate on Monday evening, do you know it?' she asked.

'Yes, just across from Downing Street,' he added.

'Good I'll see you there, then,' she said, with a smile that made his heart miss a beat, 'about 9 o'clock.'

He realised that he'd somehow agreed to meet her without even being formally asked. But he didn't mind. She leaned forward and very softly ran her fingers over the scar above his left eye, then picked up the tray and left.

Sitting at his desk taking stock of what had just happened, he was startled when the phone rang.

'Hello, Julian,' said Cliff Latcham, 'I've got an update on our local Nazi cell. Two days ago we intercepted a transmission to Abwehr in Holland. The boffins at Bletchley have broken the code and it's from Agent Banjo again and reads "confirm stiletto plan ready stop send supplies on schedule stop".'

There was a moment's silence.

'Is that it?' asked Bonham-Johns. 'Did you manage to locate it?'

'Well we've got it tightened down further to mid to west Cornwall, but the exact location is still elusive I'm afraid. You have to remember that the message took just a few seconds to send.'

'So that rules out concern about Devonport, doesn't it?' asked Bonham-Johns.

'Well, possibly but not definitely. The cell could be somewhere like Fowey, and that's still within easy reach of Plymouth.

'So where are they targeting? Agent Stiletto is in place and has a plan and wants supplies,' reiterated Bonham-Johns.

'What the hell does that mean? An air drop, a U-boat drop, a bombing raid, a bicycle?'

He shook his head.

'What facility in west Cornwall could be implicated in the commissioning of Tirpitz and warranted the attention of a Nazi spy ring?' he asked, exasperated. 'Perhaps they're going to try and break out west through the English Channel, but how? It really makes no sense.'

'Well whether it makes sense or not that's what the message says, Julian.'

'Yes you're right. OK, thanks, Cliff and get back to me immediately if there's any update.'

'Oh and Julian you'll be interested in this: Norwegian resistance have found two refuelling depots being constructed north east of Trondheim. The first is at Fættenfjord about twenty miles from the city and is the more advanced of the two, and they say it is within days of being commissioned. Six large bollards have been constructed offshore, and it seems they are expecting a large visitor and it's big enough to moor Tirpitz. The second is at Beitstadfjord which is about twenty miles further north east. That's still under construction but could be commissioned within the next two weeks or so. Both have three large bunker-oil tanks with a total capacity of around thirty thousand tons, with smaller tanks thought to be for other oils and lubricants.'

'Well that makes entire sense and strongly suggests she's going to sail north,' said Bonham-Johns. 'What about the defences?'

'That's the interesting point. Fættenfjord has permanent Flak installed, but at the time of surveillance they were not manned, and at Beitstadfjord they appear to have half-track mounted mobile units. The team will go in again in two days to check further, and I'm arranging some aerial recon with Briar Trevillian at MI14,' said Latcham.

Thirty minutes later, Bonham-Johns went to the Cipher Officer and picked up the classified decoded message. It confirmed that the USS Washington and USS Wichita were departing Charleston, South Carolina, on 28 December at 06.00. Further, he was to debrief Churchill, Rear Admiral Thornton and the captains of Prince of Wales and Hotspur in Devonport on 5 January. He read the message three times. Churchill had clearly mentioned he was going to discuss something with Thornton but there was no mention of that in the message. Was this another of Churchill's 'truth is so precious that she should always be attended by a bodyguard of lies'? He knew there was no point in trying to second-guess it. With that he screwed up the piece of paper and threw it in his waste paper bin. That will be a very interesting meeting, he thought.

Friday 26 December 1941 – 4.00 pm

Noordwijk, occupied Netherlands

In his listening post in Noordwijk, Holland, Klaus Wenger listened intently to a recording of the conversation. 'Pequod and Rachel arrival confirmed for replenishment. No word from Ahab.' Wenger recognised the voice of Colonel Bonham-Johns. 'I can confirm Peleg and Bildad had discussions and Queequeg and Tashtego depart tomorrow for hunting ground.' Again, Wenger recognised the gruff voice of Churchill. He always got a thrill from listening in on top secret conversations.

Wenger went through the transcript. 'I look forward to meeting Queequeg and Tashtego, but please confirm Daggoo to follow?' from Bonham-Johns. 'Negative, my boy, Daggoo not available. Peleg will meet Ahab to discuss. I need you to meet Peleg, Ahab, Starbuck and Stubb in port on fifth,' from Churchill.

This has got to be important, he thought. He didn't recognise the names. Were they code words for people or military hardware? For Churchill and his Personal Operations Liaison Officer to be talking on a known leaky line, it had to be either a red herring or something very important.

Wenger shouted to his team, 'Hey, anyone know what or who Queequeg and Tashtego are?'

There was silence and a shaking of heads. Bugger, he thought.

'What about Daggoo?'

But again there was no response. Wenger re-read the transcript.

'Listen up,' he said, 'does anyone recognise anything here?' and he read out the whole message.

'What was that first name?' asked Stefan Merensky, one of Wenger's team leaders.

'Peleg, Bildad.'

'No, the first name, Peek-something.'

'Pequod?' replied Wenger.

'Yes, I know that name. Now, what the hell is it?' and he put his head in his hands.

'It's something I've read, I think,' said Merensky, 'it'll come to me.'

'Better make it quick,' said Wenger. 'This is from a discussion with the old bulldog himself.'

'Stefan, come over here. I need you to help me on this,' said Wenger. 'Go through this transcription and get me a logic flow diagram. There's something cooking here.'

It was now clear to Wenger and his masters that Churchill had sailed from Greenock to Annapolis in Maryland on the Duke of York, but the ship had been turned around quickly and had departed the next day. This meant his return would probably be by air or less likely by an alternative ship. Berlin had cogitated on this and a return by air was considered the highest probability and presented an opportunity to assassinate Churchill on his return journey. The question was would he fly from Washington via Iceland, or Nova Scotia via the west coast of Ireland?

They had sent messages to their agents in Washington, New York, Boston and Halifax to look out for any unusual aircraft activity, particularly with the Royal Air Force, and report immediately.

Jagdgeschwader squadron 1 in Brittany and Jagdgeschwader squadron 5 in Stavanger had been put on alert. This was an ideal time to decapitate the British Government and ferment turmoil. The Fuehrer was emphatic about the opportunity and had ordered that all available assets be applied to assassinating his nemesis.

Saturday 27 December 1941 – 3.00 pm

Hvalfjörður, Iceland

Rear Admiral Thornton had just finished a telephone call with his superiors in Washington DC. The call had been on a secure line. Admiral William Leahy and Harry Hopkins, who was the President's emissary to the British Prime Minister, provided feedback on the meeting between Roosevelt and Churchill on Operation Harpoon and the agreed Allied plan to neutralise the Battleship Tirpitz.

'She is seen as the premier Nazi threat,' said Leahy, 'not just to the Brits but to the US as well and by default our Russian Allies. We can't afford to have Tirpitz loose in the Atlantic, let alone marauding along our eastern seaboard. With immediate effect we have despatched USS Washington and USS Wichita from Charleston, South Carolina, to join Operation Harpoon. They are due to refuel in Hvalfjörður in five days before sailing on to Scapa Flow to strengthen the northern North Sea blockade. The Brits are blockading the English Channel, so Tirpitz has only one way to go, and that's north.

Leonard, I want you to meet the two ships in Iceland and debrief the captains. At the moment they think they are supporting Arctic Convoy PQ7B, and, importantly, that's what we want the Nazis to think. As part of this, I want you to send a message to the Cabinet War Office in London by Hagelin code to confirm that USS Washington and USS Wichita have sailed from Charleston and are due in Hvalfjörður on the 1st January, exactly that, nothing more, nothing less. We want to keep the Nazis guessing,' said Leahy.

Not this again, thought Thornton, I'm being used as a God damn pawn.

'Yes, sir, understood,' he continued. 'The message will go out today.'

'Good,' said Leahy, 'I want you to attend a coordination meeting in Devonport, England, on the 5th January as the USA's senior representative on Operation Harpoon. Captain

Kinnenberg will take over convoy management responsibilities whilst you're away.'

'Yes, sir, I'll pass on the order,' said Thornton.

'And after that we want you to fly up to Scapa Flow and coordinate the US support of Operation Harpoon from there,' added Leahy.

By the end of the call, Thornton was a nervous wreck and his right leg was trembling in anticipation of the twelve hundred mile flight from Iceland to Plymouth in the stormiest month of the year across the North Atlantic. He was going to have many sleepless nights before then.

Sunday 28 December 1941 – 4.00 pm

Noordwijk, occupied Netherlands

Wenger was in a happy mood having received a short note back from Caja. She said she'd enjoyed the time with her parents but was glad to get back. She was so sorry he had been unwell and blamed the food served at the inn. Her friend was still away and only due back on the 7th, so they could spend New Year's Eve there. Again his mind wandered to the joys of sharing a small bed with the lovely Caja.

The operations team had just intercepted two important communications from the Allies. The first was a radio intercept from the Bay of Biscay. There were two unnamed British warships communicating with London, but beyond that, Wenger and his team had not been able to identify the vessels or decipher the content. It was unusual to hear that kind of chatter. If only the British used the US Hagelin code life would be so much easier, Wenger thought. He had notified Donitz in Lorient.

The second, just in, was a transmission from Rear Admiral Thornton to Whitehall in London stating that USS Washington and USS Wichita were sailing from Charlestown today, destination Hvalfjörður, as part of Operation Harpoon. Now, that is interesting, he thought.

'Hey Stefan, remember that message yesterday about Pequod, Peleg and others? Look at this new information. I think they fit together. Here you see that Washington and Wichita have sailed today.'

Merensky picked up the transcript and went back to his desk.

Wenger returned to the pile of messages he had to assess. Within a couple of minutes the quiet of the room was broken.

'Got it,' shouted Merensky and banged a sheet of paper on Wenger's desk.

'Pequod is the whaling ship in *Moby Dick*, and all these names, Queequeg, Peleg, Bildad and Daggoo, are characters.'

'What the hell is *Moby Dick*?' queried Wenger.

'Sir, it's a book by an American writer, Herman Melville, about a whaling expedition hunting the greatest whale of them all, Moby Dick.'

Wenger froze.

'Did you just say "hunting the greatest whale of them all"? Christ, show me what you've got.'

'Captain, the Pequod is a whaling ship from Nantucket, Peleg and Bildad are the owners, Ahab is the captain. From memory, Queequeg, Tashtego and Daggoo are the harpooners. Rachel, I think, is another whaling ship from Nantucket. So the message says that Peleg and Bildad, the owners, have spoken and agreed to send Queequeg and Tashtego today. My guess is that Peleg and Bildad are Churchill and Roosevelt and that Queequeg and Tashtego, the harpooners, are Washington and Wichita. They are heading to Hvalfjörður as part of Operation Harpoon, which is to catch "the greatest whale of them all", Tirpitz. It all fits, sir.'

'Jesus Christ, Stefan, I think you're onto something. But is Hvalfjörður their final destination? Are they going to sail with convoy PQ7B through to Russia or break away into the North Sea? If they're after Tirpitz, Hvalfjörður surely has to be just a refuelling stop?'

'And Peleg is going to discuss with Ahab and then meet with others "in port on 5th January". Peleg has to be Churchill. He was talking to Bonham-Johns, so he'll be there for sure, but who the hell are Ahab, Starbuck and Stubb ... and who the hell are Pequod and Rachel?' asked Wenger.

'Well in the book Ahab is a captain and Starbuck and Stubb are first and second mate,' said Merensky. There was silence.

'What if Ahab is Thornton and Churchill is going to meet with him? With the old bulldog in America, he must be flying back via Reykjavik?' suggested Wenger.

'And perhaps, captain, the radio communication today from the two British warships in the Bay of Biscay could be Pequod and Rachel?' ventured Merensky.

'So where would they be heading?' quizzed Wenger.

'It could be Devonport, Portsmouth, Chatham or some other port on the south coast. Devonport probably. It's the biggest and closest,' said Merensky.

'So if Pequod and Rachel are the two British ships we've picked up on the radio transmissions they're probably heading to Devonport for the meeting on the 5th. Starbuck and Stubb could be the two captains. They patrol the Western Approaches, and Washington and Wichita patrol the North Sea. Holy Mother of God, Stefan, I think you've got it,' said Wenger, slapping him on the back.

Wenger sent the information by Enigma to Donitz in Lorient and to Berlin. Within an hour there was a reply from Donitz: 'attention captain klaus wenger military intelligence noordwijk stop urgent stop attend meeting with me in pontchateau 11 am tomorrow to review surveillance stop flight arranged from venlo at 8 pm today to lorient stop'.

'Better get your skates on, captain. You have less than three hours to catch the flight,' said Merensky.

Damn it, thought Wenger. He hoped he would make it back for Wednesday night and the promised delights of Caja.

Monday 29 December 1941 – 2.00 pm

Cabinet War Rooms, London

Deep below ground in the Cabinet War Rooms, Julian Bonham-Johns was in conference with Brigadier Clifford Latcham of British Intelligence, Colonel Briar Trevillian of MI14 Photographic Intelligence and Air Vice-Marshall Sir Cedric Pike of RAF Coastal Command.

'Gentlemen,' said Bonham-Johns, 'we are coming to a critical juncture in the war with Germany. Our intelligence reports that the battleship Tirpitz is now within a few days of being commissioned and, let me assure you, she has the potential to change the course of the war. First prize is to destroy her but she is so well protected our chances of doing that in the short term are remote. What we have to do is degrade her support on as many fronts as possible, and that will provide us the opportunity to go for the kill. So, gentlemen, that's what I want to discuss with you today: Operation Harpoon.'

Everyone in the room sensed the gravity of the situation; all eyes were on Bonham-Johns.

'Based on the latest intelligence, we believe that when she leaves Wilhelmshaven she'll be joined by destroyers Richard Beitzen, Paul Jakobi, and Bruno Heinemann and sail up through the North Sea to attack the Arctic Convoys taking shelter and replenishing in one of the Norwegian fjords. Brigadier Latcham's men in Norway have identified two newly constructed refuelling facilities northeast of Trondheim and, Sir Cedric, we need to call on your resources to destroy them. Colonel Trevillian has the latest aerial reconnaissance photos to help us work out the right strategy. Briar, can I ask you to take us through them?'

'Thank you, Julian. Sir Cedric, these photos were taken yesterday at two locations, Fættenfjord and Beitstadfjord, both offshoots of the main Trondheim Fjord about twenty and forty nautical miles northeast of the city respectively. The first set is from Fættenfjord. Here we see the three large bunker fuel tanks, and there are four smaller ones along this side for other fuels and lubricants. These buildings are probably for storing munitions and other supplies. This is the berth where small freighters off-load and, if you look here you can see one docked and transferring its cargo. In this enlargement you can see six massive bollards for berthing a large vessel. The big tanks can hold about thirty thousand tons of bunker fuel, enough to refuel Tirpitz and her three escorts in one go,' said Trevillian.

'These photos are of the Beitstadfjord facility. This is laid out in a similar way with the same sized tanks, storage and berthing bollards, but as you can see it is more protected, with large mountains on three sides. If we look back at Fættenfjord, you can see this mountain behind the facility. It's the biggest of them all, but there are aerial approach options both up and down the fjord.'

'What about the anti-aircraft facilities?' asked Sir Cedric.

'I can answer that, Sir Cedric,' said Latcham.

'My team have closely inspected both facilities. At Beitstadfjord the only guns appear to be fifteen half-track mounted mobile units. This might be because they feel the site is naturally well protected by the mountains. Fættenfjord is a different story. They appear to have installed Flak 88 units right along the shoreline, and it's a bit like a hornet's nest.'

Sir Cedric stood up and walked to a large map of Europe on the conference room wall.

'So Trondheim Fjord is here and that's about six hundred nautical miles from RAF Lossiemouth in Scotland. That's our closest base. We could certainly mount an attack with Wellington bombers from 9 Squadron. But what do you want to take out as a priority, Julian? One or both facilities?'

'Sir Cedric, if we take out just one of the two facilities, we then know the ships will have to refuel at the other. They will have no option. If we take out both facilities the Germans will have to make an alternate plan and we'll be on the back foot.'

'Yes, but if we take out both facilities Tirpitz and its destroyer escort will have nowhere to refuel and they'll be sitting ducks,' suggested Sir Cedric.

'Well, sir, there are hundreds of fishing villages and towns along the Norwegian coast. All of them have fuel supplies for their fishing and cargo fleets but admittedly small in volume. We'd end up playing hide and seek along thousands of miles of fjords. I favour taking out the one facility, forcing Tirpitz and her escorts to use the other. Then at least we will know for sure where she will be at some point in time so we can mount an attack. Given the two locations, Sir Cedric, which one would give you the highest likelihood of destroying Tirpitz?'

'That's a bit like Russian roulette,' said Sir Cedric, scratching his chin. 'There's no doubt that Beitstadfjord has the most difficult approach, so notwithstanding the anti-aircraft capability I'd say the highest chance of success would be at Fættenfjord because its more exposed.'

'That makes sense,' said Bonham-Johns. 'Gentlemen, it sounds as though we have a plan to attack the Beitstadfjord facility?'

He looked around the room. Everyone nodded in agreement.

'So, Julian, what's the timing on this?' asked Sir Cedric.

'Ideally it would be when Tirpitz has sailed from Wilhelmshaven. That will catch them off guard and they'd have to commit to Fættenfjord as they'd have no time to arrange an alternative location,' said Bonham-Johns.

'You understand it will be weather dependent and we'll have to attack during the day. The approach is too dangerous at night even with a full moon. Tirpitz will almost certainly sail at night in bad weather to escape our detection, and that's not difficult in January. So we'll target the attack for thirty-six hours after her confirmed sailing,' said Sir Cedric. 'We'll just have to pray for a break in the weather,' he added.

The staff car Wenger was riding in pulled up at the check point in front of the huge wrought-iron gates. The vehicle was searched, identification papers inspected and then they were off again, sweeping up the drive to Pontchâteau. Wenger gathered his papers, marched up the steps and was met at the door by the young Naval Auxiliary. Her pretty face and neat blonde hair reminded him of Caja.

'This way, Captain Wenger,' she said and led him through the grand entrance hall and into an office.

'Please be seated. Can I get you a coffee?'

'Yes please he said, do you have any food? I'm starving.'

The young girl nodded and left the room. Wenger immediately felt nervous; he'd never met Donitz and he had a fearsome reputation. He straightened his tie and brushed down his uniform that was rather rumpled after the long journey. When he'd landed late last evening there had been no transport available, and he'd spent an uncomfortable night dozing in a chair at the airfield.

The Auxiliary returned with coffee and bread and cheese.

'Is there anyone with Admiral Donitz?' he asked.

'Yes, he's with Admiral Raeder and Marshall Ritter von Greim,' she replied.

His mouth instantly dried up, and the bread and cheese he was chewing seemed to set like concrete. He took a big swig of coffee and swallowed hard. He hadn't expected this; the head of the Navy and Goring's second in command at the Luftwaffe.

Wenger was now extremely nervous as he sat and waited. His right hand holding the coffee was shaking so he put the cup down on the table so as not to draw attention.

'Can I get you another coffee?' asked the girl.

'Yes please,' he said. Although he was no longer thirsty, he thought it might help his nerves.

As she returned, the phone on the desk rang. She picked up the receiver and said, 'I'll show him in. Captain Wenger, they'll see you now.'

When Wenger entered the room the three were sat around the large mahogany table. To one side, the huge log fire burned in the biggest fireplace he had ever seen. As the lowest rank of the three officers Donitz stood up and introduced himself. Wenger gave him a military salute followed by a Nazi salute. He thought the present company would expect that of him. Donitz did the same and then introduced him to Raeder and von Greim.

'Captain, thank you for coming at such short notice. The intelligence information you sent through is of the utmost interest to us,' said Raeder. 'You seem to suggest that the Allies have a plan to attack Tirpitz, and I and my colleagues would very much like to hear about it.'

'Yes, sir,' said Wenger. 'I have written up the intelligence we have gathered and I have two copies.'

He wasn't sure who to give them to so handed both to Raeder who simply dropped them on the table in front of him.

'Continue, captain,' said Raeder.

'Admiral, we have a number of sources of information that have led us to this conclusion. Intercepted discussions between Churchill and his Personal Operations Liaison Officer, Colonel Julian Bonham-Johns, a meeting between Bonham-Johns and Rear Admiral Thornton in Iceland and radio intercepts in the Bay of Biscay. We also have information about a top secret Arctic Convoy cargo destined for Russia.'

Wenger continued. 'Our original intercept on the 23rd December was from our agent in London who indicated there was a new initiative out of Churchill's Cabinet Office called Operation Harpoon. It was ranked as a top secret and coded initiative. This was four days after Bonham-Johns met with Thornton in Hvalfjörður. We had intercepted a message from London to Norway a couple of days previous to that mentioning "harpoon", which we now believe to be Operation Harpoon, so Norway is part of the plan.'

'The next intercept was a subsequent conversation between Churchill and Bonham-Johns on the 26th December,' Wenger elaborated. 'Churchill was in Washington, feeding back information on Operation Harpoon to Bonham-Johns. They were using code based upon characters in a book called *Moby Dick*, written by an American.'

'Yes, I've read it,' added Donitz.

Raeder looked less than pleased that one of his Admirals admitted to reading an American book.

'Sir, as you know, it's a book about a whaling expedition – "hunting the greatest whale of them all" – and we believe this refers to Tirpitz.'

'So you think Operation Harpoon is about a planned attack on Tirpitz?' queried Raeder.

'Yes, sir, that's right,' said Wenger looking at Donitz for support.

'When decoded, the message talked of a meeting between Peleg and Bildad that we now know referred to Churchill and Roosevelt's meeting in the White House on the 26th December. Bonham-Johns was asking the status of three US ships code named Queequeg, Tashtego and Daggoo but Roosevelt only agreed to send the first two. As it transpires, USS Washington and USS Wichita sailed from Charleston for Hvalfjörður on the 27th December, and we decoded a message to that effect from Thornton the following day. We're not sure which ship was held back, likely either USS Tuscaloosa or USS Mississippi. If I may say so, Admiral Donitz, it's an indication of the success your U-boats are having on the East Coast of the United States.'

'That's very kind of you, Wenger, but for your information USS Tuscaloosa sailed two days later in support of a North Atlantic Convoy from Nova Scotia to Liverpool!'

Wenger was acutely embarrassed at not having picked up that information and he could intuitively feel Raeder's piercing stare but he didn't look up to witness it. God damn it, how did we miss that one? he wondered.

'So Wenger, to recap, Washington and Wichita are bound for Hvalfjörður on what is part of Operation Harpoon, and Tuscaloosa is a couple of days behind them sailing in a similar direction,' said Raeder.

'Yes, sir, that appears to be the case,' said Wenger.

'What is the purpose of Washington and Wichita being in Hvalfjörður? They pose no threat to Tirpitz there. And what's the story about a top secret cargo, Wenger? It sounds rather implausible to me,' said Raeder.

'Well, sir, on the 21st December we received information from one of our contacts at Hvalfjörður that part of the manifest for Arctic Convoy PQ7B contained seventy of the latest tachometric bombsights manufactured by Norden Inc. in Indianapolis. These are for use on the B-25J Mitchell bombers the US is providing the Russians. Two days before that, on the 19th December, the same day that Bonham-Johns was there, the original convoy PQ7 was split into PQ7A and PQ7B. PQ7A then sailed with minimal escort on the 21st December. PQ7B was held back with no specific sailing date. Sir, it's got to be more than a coincidence that all this happened over such a short time period. It is possible that they're waiting for the Washington and Wichita to be on station to provide protection for the convoy.'

'Have you been to Russia, Wenger? Do you know the calibre of the Russian serviceman?' asked Raeder.

Wenger shook his head; he hadn't been to Russia.

'Well let me tell you, Wenger, they are ignorant peasants, all of them. You give a Russian a block of iron and he'll break it. Sophisticated equipment such as tachometric bombsights is a non-starter for the Russians. It's a hoax,' said Raeder. 'Carry on.'

'Sir, the second part of the discussion between Churchill and Bonham-Johns indicated that Churchill is going to meet with Thornton, presumably in Reykjavik. With Churchill currently in America and due to fly back in the next few days, that is a logical routing. He can't fly across the Atlantic in one hop.'

Raeder and von Greim looked at one another.

'Are you suggesting, Wenger, that Churchill is going to fly back to England via Iceland?' asked Raeder.

'Yes, sir, I am. That's what the information indicates.'

'And when is this flight going to occur?' asked Raeder.

'Well, sir, if he has a meeting in England on the 5th, it has to be within the next six days.'

'So, Ritter, it looks as though you might have a crack at Churchill. Is that possible if he flies from Iceland to London?'

'Yes it is. The Messerschmitt 109s of Jagdgeschwader squadron 5 in Stavanger have the range and capability. The key will be good ground intelligence. We can't patrol the skies over the North Atlantic twenty-four hours a day – it has to be specifically targeted. Give us his day of departure and we'll get him,' said von Greim.

Raeder nodded.

'So what about this meeting in England, Wenger?' asked Raeder.

'Sir, they are both going to meet "with others" in port on the 5th January and we're confident that's going to be Devonport. We know that Thornton is going to be there because we decoded one of his transmissions. We have been puzzling over Starbuck and Stubb. In the book they are first and second mate. Pequod and Rachel are ships and we believe that they are likely the two British ships we've got a radio fix on in the Bay of Biscay.'

'So again to recap,' said Raeder, 'in a couple of days there will be two British Battleships guarding the Western English Channel. Washington and Wichita will be at Hvalfjörður with Tuscaloosa God-knows-where?'

'That's what the information suggests, sir,' said Wenger.

'Donitz, it's of paramount importance we find out who the two British ships are. We need to know what we're up against here.'

'Yes, sir, it will be organised immediately. We have U-552 leaving today for the Irish Sea,' said Donitz.

'And Ritter, if we don't get Churchill in the air what about a fireworks reception for the *Moby Dick* characters on the 5th?'

'Erich, I have a large raid planned for Devonport Dockyard on the 3rd. I can delay it two days,' said Ritter von Greim with a smile.

'So that leaves Washington and Wichita ... what the hell are they up to?' Raeder mused.

'Sir, I'd stake my reputation on them providing protection for PQ7B. Our contact has never been wrong before,' said Wenger, feeling emboldened.

'Your reputation, eh?' queried Raeder. 'If you're wrong it'll cost you more than that, and I'd stake my reputation on that.'

Wenger wasn't sure if he was being mocked or threatened, but either way he didn't like the sound of it. He just stared at the floor.

'Thank you, Wenger,' said Donitz. 'Stay around today in case we need you further and notify us the second any new information is received.'

With that, the briefing was over.

Wenger was relieved at the apparent short duration of his trip. At this rate he hoped to back in Noordwijk tomorrow night in plenty of time to take Caja out on Wednesday.

Monday 29 December 1941 – 8.50 pm

Cabinet War Rooms, London

For the last couple of hours Julian Bonham-Johns had tried to concentrate on the task in hand, but his mind kept wandering to thoughts of Lucy. What was it about that girl? he mused. He'd never had such immediate and intimate feelings before.

He focused on reading through the intelligence report on Agent Stiletto and the possible targets. He looked at the list and worked through the pros and cons of each being associated with the escape of Tirpitz and the potential target for the Nazi cell. Surely it had to be a military facility? Number one on the list was the top secret radar system network known as Chain Home, the codename for the ring of coastal early warning radar stations to detect and track aircraft. This had become a critical asset which allowed the British Fighter Command to identify and engage incoming German bomber formations. Counting the number of radar facilities in Cornwall alone, Bonham-Johns came to twenty three. They can't attack all of them at once, but which one would they go after? he thought. Losing one or two would not bring the system down.

One name on the list appeared twice: RAF Portreath. It was an established RAF radar station and a Fighter Command station that had recently received a number of Hudson bombers from 59 Squadron. They were testing the new long range anti-submarine ASV radar along the English Channel and as far south as the Bay of Biscay. So could that be the potential target? If the ASV radar was destroyed, Tirpitz and her escort could be supported by a flotilla of U-boats as they made their bid to escape west.

But this was just one of a myriad of well defended military installations, and what could one or two agents hope to achieve? Porthcurno Telegraph Station was strategically important, but what possible implication could there be with Tirpitz? Bonham-Johns brushed his hair back. He still had a feeling that Devonport Dockyard was the target, but why, when and exactly how he didn't know.

He put the papers down on the table and rubbed his face and eyes to regain focus. He glanced at the small clock on his desk and smiled; it was time to go. He put on his thick coat, locked his office door, and walked down the corridor and looked at the weather board; it read 'Freezing Fog'. He grimaced at the thought.

He climbed the two flights of steps to the exit, the guards opened the door and it was as though he'd walked into a black curtain. He could see nothing. He closed his eyes for several seconds and then when more accustomed to the dark could just start to make out his surroundings. After the sterile air of his subterranean home the stench of the war-torn city hit his nostrils. It was a mixture of cordite, sewage, acrid smoke and something altogether more unpleasant. He pulled the torch from his pocket and walked off into the thick 'pea-souper' fog.

As he crossed Parliament Street, Big Ben boomed out nine o'clock in a deep melancholy peal as if to echo the gloom of the war-weary winter's night. Within a couple of minutes he was at The Red Lion pub and opened the door and entered through the blackout curtain.

He looked around and saw Lucy sitting alone, and she smiled radiantly when she saw him.

'I thought you were with friends?' he ventured.

'Oh they couldn't make it, I'm afraid you're stuck with me,' she said, offering her hand.

'I thought I might have missed you as I had to nip home and have a bath and put on some clean clothes and contact my neighbour – she was worried because she hadn't heard from me. You know we were all held at the Cabinet War Rooms for 48 hours when The Boss departed for the USA the other day. I hadn't realised they did that. Did you?' she asked.

'Yes I did, actually,' said Bonham-Johns, but his mind was captivated by her beauty. She was wearing a tight blue woollen jumper with a long pearl necklace. She looks absolutely gorgeous, thought Bonham-Johns.

When he realised he was staring at where the necklace fell, he asked, 'Uh what can I get you to drink, Lucy?'

'Can I have a gin and pink, please?'

'You certainly can. I'll be right back.'

When he returned with the drinks she gave him one of her disarming smiles.

'Are you married?' she said out of the blue, catching Bonham-Johns completely off guard. He looked at her quizzically.

'Sorry, me and my big mouth,' she said, 'always putting my foot in it.'

'That's alright,' said Bonham-Johns, 'I am, but we're separated, have been for nearly a year. Too much time apart and all that sort of thing.'

He couldn't believe he was confiding in someone he hardly knew about his private life, and changed the subject.

'And what about you?' he said.

'Oh you know, the odd boyfriend here and there, but I can't take the uncertainty of them not coming back. So many lovely young men killed for this war,' she said sadly.

'Well, we're not through that yet. We have many difficult days ahead,' he said imitating Churchill's voice.

'You sound just like him,' she laughed, and their eyes engaged for several seconds.

'I know nothing about you, Lucy,' said Bonham-Johns as much to break the moment as anything else.

'Oh, not much to tell really. I was born in London but spent my childhood in South Africa. My father was a writer. He was born out there, and when he and my Mum were— well, when they died, I was sent back here to boarding school. I went to St Wilfrid's School in Exeter.'

'So you were here all alone?'

'Pretty much. I did have an aunt who used to visit me at school very occasionally, but bless her, she always remembered to send me something for my birthday.'

'So how come you're in the Cabinet War Rooms?' asked Bonham-Johns.

'Well, I wanted to do my bit and joined the WAAFs initially, but I wanted something more interesting.'

Bonham-Johns couldn't help smiling.

'I know what you're thinking: "but you're just a waitress". But the truth is I like making coffee for The Boss. I really feel I'm contributing to the war effort. If Mr Churchill's not happy then we're all in trouble aren't we? Right?'

She engaged him with one of her disarming smiles. Bonham-Johns wanted to touch her, take her in his arms and hug her. She seemed so vulnerable but in control at the same time; and that smile. Again he realised he was staring at her and making a fool of himself.

He grabbed his glass, finished off the last of the beer and said, 'I need a refill. How about you, Lucy?'

'Oh yes please,' she said, adding 'it's helping me relax.'

Bonham-Johns waited at the crowded bar and was chatting to some American army officers he knew. Lucy took a piece of paper from her bag and scribbled a note. When Bonham-Johns returned with the drinks she slipped the pen and paper back into her bag.

'Oh, thanks,' she said and sipped her new drink. 'So what do you do for Churchill? You didn't tell me last time,' she asked, again surprising Bonham-Johns with her direct approach. A bit strange, he thought, as nearly everyone in the Cabinet War Rooms knew his role.

'I keep him supplied with cigars and brandy,' he said. 'As you say, got to keep The Boss happy.'

'Touché,' she said with a smile. 'Seriously though Julian you seem to be able to get his attention at short notice.'

'Have you seen him without a cigar?' quipped Bonham-Johns. 'So where do you live, then? when you're not buried beneath Whitehall?' he asked, trying to change the subject.

'In Pitts Head Street actually, in Mayfair,' she said.

'Well well, that's a posh address,' he added, still tempted to reach forward and touch her hand.

'I live there on my own. It's rather lonely actually,' she said, looking straight into his eyes. He smiled at her and reached forward and covered her hand with his. It felt so good, so full of promise.

He was about to suggest dinner in the West End that weekend when the air raid sirens sounded across the city, to the annoyance of Bonham-Johns and everyone in the pub. With muttering and swearing, people started to quickly leave.

'Oh no, that's not fair is it? Come on, we need to get back to base,' he said, and they ran hand-in-hand back to the Cabinet War Rooms.

Just short of the sandbagged door she stopped and pulled Bonham-Johns towards her.

'That was a wonderful evening,' she whispered passionately. 'Here's my phone number. Give me a call when you're free.' And with that, she handed him a piece of paper and gave him a lingering kiss on the lips with just the faintest touch of her tongue.

'Remember: Mayfair 3349,' she said, 'any time.'

The touch of her tongue on his lips was like a bolt of electricity flowing through him. Bonham-Johns was riveted to the spot with the unexpected delight. In the distance the first anti-aircraft guns started up, breaking the spell and forcing them back into their subterranean lodgings.

Tuesday 30 December 1941 – 5.00 am

The Final Sweep, Porthcurno

In the early hours of the morning the Stranger had been woken by hail stones rattling against his bedroom window. He flashed the torch at his watch. It was an hour earlier than he'd planned to get up but he was awake now. He went downstairs, lit the oil lamp and stoked the Cornish Range and put the kettle on top. With a steaming hot cup of sugary black tea he tucked into a plate of cold rabbit stew and a boiled egg.

He had a busy morning ahead of him checking in detail the exact route of the planned mission. He prided himself on attention to detail. With the hailstones still beating against the window he knew it was going to be a cold and wet one. He was edgy and on high alert after the debacle at Boswednack Farm. When he'd returned to Fern Cottage later that evening he'd found both the front and back trip wires broken.

After packing some food and a flask of the remaining tea he left the cottage. He checked the light trip wires he'd reset last night and found them intact. Quietly he locked the back door, stepped over the wire and disappeared into the darkness. Keeping to the lee of the hedge he avoided the worst of the hail and sleet showers that were being driven across the exposed peninsula. Even so, his coat was soon soaked and he contemplated a cold, miserable morning.

Twenty minutes later he had reached the Porthcurno Road above Boscarn Hamlets and he lay behind the hedge and listened. He knew there were two pill boxes about fifty yards up the road to his left and he had to avoid these at all costs. Satisfied there was no one approaching, half-crouched, he slipped quickly across the road and leapt over the five bar gate opposite with a single spring. He untied the rope that kept the gate shut and retied it to look as though it still had purpose. That would enable an easy opening of the gate for those carrying heavy backpacks. That was the first hurdle behind him.

Moving more quickly, he worked south along the hedge by the

road. Coming to a fence he peered over and saw the row of back gardens behind the terraced houses of Boscarn Hamlets. He jumped the fence and counted the houses. Outside the back gate to number three he quietly clicked the latch and the gate swung open. To the right was a chicken coop and his unexpected presence got the cockerel excited and it started a raucous warning. With all the houses in darkness he quickly opened the door to the coop and cornered the alarmed bird. Grabbing it by the wing and trying to avoid the flailing spurs he snapped its neck, closed the coop door and disappeared into the thicket behind the houses. At a safe distance he took stock of the situation. Several minutes later no lights had come on and all was quiet. Whilst the back of his hand had been slashed by a spur, he now had something tasty for supper and he'd got rid of a potentially noisy guard at one of their target locations.

This had been well worth his while. Attention to detail always pays, he thought. Hiding the dead bird high up in the hedge and out the way of foxes, he continued south on his next mission.

Staying close to a hedge he cautiously moved forward. After a few minutes he could make out the sandbagged gun emplacement covered in camouflage netting. It was directly above the Telegraph Station and he needed to confirm its purpose. Crawling on his belly he inched forward across the open field. Half way across the heavens opened again and hail stones stung his face. With no shelter he was soaked further but the noise afforded him extra cover so he sprinted the last few yards and dropped down against the northern wall.

With hailstones still pelting down, he risked a quick look over the edge. To his right a mounted machine gun pointed out over the valley but he could see no soldiers. He snatched another look and in the centre he saw a large concrete structure with a heavy gauge steel bar door on the northern side. Warm moist air rose from the door and could be seen as wisps of mist as it condensed in the cold air. That's it, he thought, well pleased with himself. That confirms it's the connection with the underground facility.

As quickly as it had started the hail storm stopped. It was suddenly quiet and all he could hear was the thumping beat of his heart. Then he heard voices and tried to listen to the conversation but could not pick up what they were saying. He peered cautiously again and saw two soldiers with their backs to him looking out over the valley. He took the opportunity to further study the emplacement. To one side of the concrete structure the soldiers had a tarpaulin 'lean-to' to provide shelter from the elements. The camouflage net over the whole emplacement was for anonymity not shelter.

He could see some wafts of steam coming from under the tarpaulin and it was clear they had a small stove for making hot drinks and warming food. There was also a radio crackling quietly in the background.

Satisfied with his surveillance he checked one more time and the soldiers were still in deep conversation. Keeping low and moving quickly he made to the cover of some bushes and in the lee of the hedge he worked back towards Boscarn Hamlets to pick up the cockerel and return to Fern Cottage for an unexpected feast.

Wednesday 31 December 1941 – 11.00 am
Pontchâteau, France

Dettsmann arrived at the Château at 10.50 am. This time the young Auxiliary at the desk gave him a warm smile when he entered the office.

'Please wait,' she said, 'they'll see you shortly.'

I wonder who 'they' are, he thought.

When he entered, Admiral Raeder was seated at the head of the table with two other senior officers.

'Come over here, Dettsmann,' said Raeder, 'let me introduce you: Colonel Bernard Frolich of the National Intelligence Agency and Lieutenant Commander Herbert Schultze, second in command of 7th U-boat flotilla based down the road in St Nazaire.'

They saluted and then shook hands.

'At our last meeting, Dettsmann, I told you that we needed a diversionary tactic, a very bold one,' said Raeder. 'What we are about to tell you is of the utmost secrecy, do you understand?'

'Yes, Admiral,' Dettsmann replied with a rather dry throat.

Frolich unrolled a map and laid it out on the table in front of them. It was a large map and it showed red lines running from the south western tip of England to different points all around the world, like long, thin, red octopus tentacles. At the top of the map the title read 'Cable and Wireless Great Circle Map 1939'.

'Dettsmann, this is Porthcurno Telegraph Station in the centre and these red lines are submarine communication cables,' said Frolich. 'They connect Britain to its empire and beyond; Canada, USA, South Africa, India, South East Asia, Australia and New Zealand. They're armoured cables six inches in diameter that lie at the bottom of the ocean, and there's about one hundred and fifty thousand miles of them in total.'

Dettsmann looked incredulous. 'How long did that take to put down?' he asked.

'The first one was laid in the 1870s, and they've been adding to it ever since. The starting point in England is here at the village of

Porthcurno in Cornwall,' he tapped his cane on the spot. 'All these red lines, and there are currently fourteen of them, represent an electronic communication network connecting Britain with the world. Its security is so important that not only is special attention given to its defence, but the operations and critical components have recently been relocated deep underground.'

'From this facility we believe they are capable of communicating up to seventy-five thousand words an hour; indeed they are communicating most of their war effort through this single facility. They receive messages from London and around Britain and then forward transmit to the required destination. Each location has a unique call sign. The War Office, the Admiralty and the War Cabinet, including Churchill, all have their vital communications routing through Porthcurno. Seventy-five percent of all their secure International communications go through this one facility.'

'It's a sophisticated system. Outgoing messages are received from around Britain by conventional Morse code communication or by mail sacks flown in daily and then typed out on punched tape called slip. Messages can be typed on a standard typewriter to create the punched tape. Some of these messages are already encrypted when received, and others are encrypted at Porthcurno to provide added security. The slip is then fed into an automatic transmitter that reads punched holes and sends them down the cables as electronic pulses. In a matter of seconds a message can be in New Zealand.'

'Sir, that is amazing intelligence for such a top secret site,' ventured Dettsmann.

'Yes, indeed. We have one of our best operatives on the ground there, in fact he's your contact on arrival,' replied Frolich.

He pulled out another plan and laid it on top of the first.

'As you can imagine, the facility is very well defended,' he said, again pointing with his cane. 'The cable station is located in a steep-sided valley containing the village of Porthcurno with a beach at the bottom overlooked by two hundred and fifty foot high granite cliffs. A road runs down the valley through the village, before turning west towards St. Levan. The northern boundary of the village is at Boscarn Hamlets, marked by this turn in the road. Our man on the ground has provided good intelligence. Some three hundred troops from the 11th Battalion West Yorkshire Regiment and 7th Battalion Duke of Cornwall's Light Infantry are stationed in the area. Our intelligence suggests there are twelve pillboxes, six security bunkers with an assortment of Bren guns, anti-tank mortars and Bofors anti-aircraft installations.'

'The facility is located deep underground entered via two blast-proof and gas-proof doors, and the whole area is surrounded by an unscalable electrified fence, floodlights and flame throwers. Access is through two security checkpoints before you get to the tunnels and is strictly limited to those with special ID cards.'

'Interestingly,' he said, with a knowing grin, 'for emergency evacuation, a covert emergency escape route is provided by steps cut into a steeply inclined tunnel leading from the rear of the underground facility to a well-fortified exit in the fields above.'

'Colonel,' said Dettsmann, 'if we want to destroy it why don't we use bombers to obliterate the area?'

'Ah yes we could do, we've looked at that, but that would only damage the cables on surface and they can be replaced. What we must do is destroy the underground instrument room – that will put them out of action for many months rather than a few days.'

'Your mission, code name Operation Cut-Throat, is to rendezvous with our man on the ground, gain access and destroy the equipment,' said Frolich. 'You have handpicked four troopers and they are ready?'

'Yes, sir. Fit, trained and ready to go,' said Dettsmann.

'Good, I want your team to report for duty at St Nazaire submarine pen tomorrow for final preparations.'

As Dettsmann turned to leave, Raeder said, 'Oh and one last thing, before you destroy the Telegraph facility, and this is the crucial point, Dettsmann, I need you to send a message. Your contact will communicate this to you.'

Wednesday 31 December 1941 – 8.00 pm
De Oude Molen Inn, Noordwijk

Being New Year's Eve the inn was packed with German soldiers. It was one of their favourite haunts and the owner was very obliging. Given the austerity of the war, having well paid German troops filling his inn was good business.

There were also a number of locals enjoying the celebration and a few Dutch girls intent on helping to lighten the German soldier's pockets. Caja walked into the inn and looked around for Klaus Wenger. As she walked across to the bar she received unwelcome attention from a number of drunken soldiers. She was fondled, had her backside touched and was kissed on the lips. She was sickened by the base behaviour of what she and her comrades classified as Nazi scum.

She asked the barman if he'd seen her date but he shook his head. He poured her a glass of the house wine and she stood to one side of the bar with her back to the wall. One hour and three glasses later she had given up on him.

She'd been looking around at the German officers in the room and had identified one senior officer who she'd caught staring at her. With one last check for Wenger she walked across to her new target, sat down at the table and started to chat.

After several more large glasses of schnapps, one with a tiny white pill slipped into it, the German officer was suddenly not feeling so good and went to the toilet. On his return he was slurring his words, kissed her clumsily and fondled her in a less than discrete way.

Caja whispered into his ear that she had a room where they could go.

'Lead the way "mijn mooie jonge hoer",' he said, and unsteadily followed her out of the inn. They stopped in several doorways where she let his hands explore her body.

Glancing around to see that all was clear, she directed him down a side-alley and unlocked a door.

'This is where I stay, my room is through here,' she whispered in his ear.

Opening the door, the large, drunk officer followed her in and didn't see the man waiting in a side-room, he was too preoccupied with what was about to happen. He knew nothing of the iron bar that crunched into the back of his skull. The man who wielded the bar closed and locked the door, pulled out a short length of rope, looped it around the German's neck and with a knee in the middle of his back pulled hard on the ends of the rope, strangling the remaining life from him.

'It's not the Abwehr captain, Jan. He didn't show,' said Caja. 'This is the most senior officer I could get.'

'Shit, that's too bad, we really want to get him but good work anyway, Caja,' said Jan. 'One less Nazi scumbag.'

Between them, they dragged the lifeless officer out into the back yard. Jan pulled a torch from his pocket and flashed it down the lane, and within seconds a blacked-out car pulled up. He searched the officer for valuables, ID papers and pistol and gave them to Caja. Jan and the driver grabbed the body and threw it unceremoniously into the boot.

'Good work but you shouldn't go back to the inn for a few days, and don't get caught with those personal effects, Caja,' said the driver, and drove off into the night.

Caja returned to the house, bolted the back door and left via the front door, locked it and headed home.

Thursday 1 January 1942 – 2.00 pm

South Western Approaches, English Channel

U-552 sat on the sea bed three hundred and twenty feet below the surface of the South Western Approaches, thirty nautical miles south of Plymouth Sound. With all equipment including the ventilation shut down, it was hot, humid and smelly. There was complete silence apart from the ping-ping of the sonar stalking them. Ping-ping, silence, ping-ping. The crew were used to the rhythm and knew it would repeat but each time it did, they still twitched. They couldn't help themselves. The balance between life and death on a hunted submarine was measured in the time a depth charge could be dropped on them; at that depth, about thirty seconds.

Ping-ping, but this time slightly less intense, or was it their imagination? Ping-ping, and yes it was now perceptibly less intense. Wet foreheads were wiped with relief and the marble like expressions of the crew eased. The captain, Erich Rohne, gesticulated for the crew to remain silent. It was not over.

Radio Petty Officer Willem Ewald was listening intently, clasping his headphones against his ears, his eyes tightly closed, periodically tuning one of the two dials on the hydrophone in front of him. He could hear the throbbing screws of the British ship and was focusing on the signature of the engine and propellers, an H-class destroyer if he wasn't mistaken. He paged through the enemy ship identification book in front of him and was flicking between two pages. There was a distinctive arrhythmia to the signal indicating a damaged propeller blade. He listen intently for another minute and then confidently scribbled down 'HMS Hotspur, H-class destroyer' and passed it to the captain who smiled and slapped him on the shoulder. He now had a positive identification.

Twenty agonising minutes later the pinging had stopped. Ewald scribbled a new note: 'new larger ship ten thousand yards west, moving northeast'. The crew anticipated action but Captain Rohne raised his hand for silence. Plymouth was home to the

114

largest Naval Base in Britain, Devonport Dockyard, and to be this close was akin to poking at a hornet's nest with a matchstick. Ewald passed another message: 'ship seven thousand yards northwest moving east'.

'Ya,' said Rohne, 'time to move, blow tanks,' and with a rush of air the submarine shook itself free from the sea bed.

'Half ahead, 20 degrees up.'

The crew sensed they were on the hunt.

As the periscope broke surface, Rohne did a full 360-degree sweep of the horizon. The large ship Ewald had heard was clear to see on the horizon steaming towards Devonport and safety.

'Ya, full ahead, bearing 350 degrees, down to two hundred feet,' said Rohne, 'right, let's find out who you are.'

U-552 sped towards its target.

'Six thousand yards and closing, captain,' reported Ewald.

'Any fix?' asked Rohne.

Ewald listened intently and paged through the enemy ship identification book before replying.

'Captain, I'm pretty sure it's a King George V class battleship. Four screws, Parsons-geared turbines and definite synchronous harmonic – it has to be a battleship.

'Ya, good work, Willem. Let's get some photos, back to periscope depth.'

As he focused the periscope he felt distinctly uneasy. At just over five thousand yards silhouetted against the light blue sky of the sinking sun there she was, the British Battleship, but where the hell was her escort? Why was she alone? He hesitated a couple of seconds whilst he took a series of photos and gave the order to arm and load two torpedoes.

'Starboard ten degrees. Distance?'

'Four thousand five hundred, captain,' said Ewald.

'Torpedoes set, ya, fire one,' and the submarine shuddered slightly as its lethal cargo departed.

'Starboard five,' he ordered, 'fire two,' and with that he did a 360 degree sweep with the periscope.

'Shit, dive, dive, dive, enemy aircraft, thirty degrees down, full ahead. Depth to the sea bed?'

'Just short of four hundred feet, captain,' came the reply.

The U-boat creaked and groaned as the pressure built rapidly on the hull.

'Sir, the target has turned – I think she's onto us,' shouted Ewald to be heard above the noise of frantic activity.

'Port 90 degrees, maintain full speed,' Rohne said.

'Aircraft depth charge in the water,' shouted Ewald. 'Now two, three, four in the water.'

'Depth?'

'Two fifty-five, captain.'

'Where's the bottom?'

'Another one hundred, captain.'

'Ya engines half, maintain thirty degrees down.'

'Bottom?'

'Fifty feet, captain, closing fast.'

'Ya ten degrees up, engines stop.'

The crew grabbed hold of whatever they could as U-552 crunched violently into the seabed, rasping and scraping over the rocks and boulders before she settled.

'Damn it,' thought Rohne, 'they must have heard that.'

He'd been hoping for soft sand.

The thud of the first depth charge exploded far away, the second much closer, the third closer again and the fourth rocked the submarine and hit it like a sledge hammer. The crew rubbed their ears from the pressure burst.

'Ya, blow oil and debris tank, complete silence.'

Rohne had successfully used the debris tank on four previous occasions, but would this yet again fool the hunter?

'Depth charges in the water, four of them,' whispered Ewald, 'torpedoes have missed their target, captain.'

They waited in complete silence for what seemed an eternity, but to their relief the four depth charges exploded at a safe distance. The crew all grinned and gave the captain a thumbs-up.

'Battleship three thousand yards and closing,' whispered Ewald.

'Shit,' said Rohne, 'complete silence, full shutdown.'

As the fans switched off the heat rocketed and within minutes they all had sweat dripping from them. 'Fifteen hundred yards and closing,' scribbled Ewald.

The next message read one thousand yards, the next five hundred. The entire crew was staring at Ewald. Close to panic, he gesticulated that depth charges were in the water. He started to try and communicate the number but lost count in the cacophony of them hitting the water. They all braced for oblivion.

The submarine was buffeted by shockwaves time and time again, some of the crew crying out in terror at the maelstrom. But when the last depth charge had exploded they were still alive, the submarine intact, as far as they could tell. Rohne looked at Ewald but he shrugged his shoulders and indicated the hydrophones were broken.

'Shit,' muttered Rohne and indicated to the crew to stay silent. He then went around to each man and enquired with facial expression if they were alright, a friendly slap on the cheek given to reassure them.

After fifteen minutes' silence Rohne said, 'Ya, blow tanks and half ahead, two hundred feet, one eight zero. Good work, men. HMS Hotspur and a King George V class battleship positively identified with photographs for confirmation. Let's get out of here, send some messages and get back to St Nazaire.'

The crew cheered and hugged one another and sang. It was so good to be alive.

Friday 2 January 1942 – 2.00 pm

Noordwijk, occupied Netherlands

Wenger had languished in Lorient for three days and as a consequence he'd missed his night out with Caja on Wednesday. That was the second time he'd missed the opportunity to sleep with her, and he was really fed up.

He'd had one further meeting with Donitz to update him on the movements of Washington and Wichita and to report that HMS Duke of York and three escorts had been sighted by a U-boat nearly five hundred miles south of Newfoundland heading south at full speed. This, he suggested to Donitz, indicated that it was going to collect Churchill and return him to England. But even with that information he'd got the distinct impression he was no longer of importance and was shunted from one office to another trying to arrange a flight back to Venlo. However, the accommodation and tasty French food had been very much to his liking.

The first thing he did when he landed was get the staff car to make a turn by De Oude Molen so he could leave a message for Caja. He was concerned she'd think he'd stood her up. But then she was so generous and loving the last time they met surely she would understand. He explained that he had had to fly to Nantes for a top-level meeting and said he hoped she'd forgive him and asked when he could see her again.

When he walked into the Operations Room the team smiled, and Stefan Merensky welcomed him back.

'So how was the mighty Admiral?' he asked.

'Oh you know, made me coffee, cleaned my boots, things like that,' Wenger joked.

'Right, Stefan, bring me up to date on Operation Harpoon communications.'

'Well, captain, yesterday we intercepted a message from Thornton reporting that Washington and Wichita are on their way to Scapa Flow. Their departure was confirmed by our contact in Hvalfjörður, but he also reports that Convoy PQ7B is still in the harbour.'

'That surely means that the convoy is a red herring after all,' said Wenger. 'Did you communicate that?'

'Yes, captain, we sent that through to Donitz and Berlin yesterday when we received it.'

Oh God, so much for my reputation, he thought, and remembering the threat issued by Admiral Raeder he suddenly had an unpleasant tingling sensation in his belly.

'Also there's been no sign of Churchill in Hvalfjörður or any unusual air traffic. That has to mean that Churchill is returning to England on HMS Duke of York,' said Merensky.

With that additional information the tingling turned into a churning. How the hell can all that intelligence, coming from reliable sources, end up being a complete lie? he wondered. He shook his head in disbelief.

'Oh yes and we intercepted a communication between U-552 and Donitz. The two British ships that we picked up in the Bay of Biscay are the Hotspur and Prince of Wales and they're now in Devonport,' said Merensky.

'Well at least I got something right,' mumbled Wenger.

Saturday 3 January 1942 – 10.00 am

St Nazaire, France

'Ah, Dettsmann, come in,' said Colonel Bernard Frolich who he'd met three days before. 'This is Kapitänleutnant Karl Thurmann of U-553. He's going to take you and your platoon to the target rendezvous.'

Thurmann walked over and gave Dettsmann a firm handshake, and there was an immediate camaraderie between them. Both were front line heroes and both wore the iron cross.

Dettsmann introduced the four troopers: 'This is Sergeant Carl Krueger, Corporal Herman Baecker, and Privates Gert Fischer and Niklas Hanke.'

All clicked their heels as they saluted, chests out, proudly wearing their grey caps with edelweiss emblems. They were all young, with Krueger being the oldest at twenty one. All had had tough and troubled childhoods in the slums of Hamburg and had been easy pickings for the fanatical leaders of the Nazi party. Members of the party since their early teens, they had been fast-tracked to a brutal career in the 3rd Mountain Division. Thurmann eyed them with disdain.

'Welcome to Operation Cut-Throat,' he said, and with that rolled out a map of west Cornwall on the huge table. They all clustered around, eager to see their target. The map was heavily colour-coded.

'This red area along the coast indicates that the sea and the beaches are mined,' said Thurmann.

That doesn't give us many options, thought Dettsmann, but he kept the thought to himself.

'Here is your target, Dettsmann – Porthcurno and the Telegraph Station. We want to get you as close as we can but as you see it's tricky. Our intelligence tells us that there is a network of sonar stations right around here to guard the cables against submarine attack. The beaches are protected by mines ... access to the cliffs might be possible but they're almost impossible to climb – near-vertical and slick with clay and loose rock.'

To the east of your target, Cripps Cove and Penberth Cove are both heavily mined and impossible to access. Porthguarnon, further to the east, is a distinct possibility for a dinghy landing but you would need to take a long detour north around the village of Treen to get to your target. That would waste valuable time and increase the likelihood of being caught.'

'To the west from Minack Point around Gwennap Head and up to Boswednack Island there are no landing locations because of the Atlantic breakers and the sheer cliffs. Further north there are heavy defences associated with the Sennen wireless and RAF Station. There is, however,' he added, looking closer at the plan, 'a chance that we can get you ashore here, at the southern end of Nanjizal Bay. It's heavily mined but there appears to be a narrow, clear channel that you might get through in a non-magnetic rubber dinghy. The local fishermen used it until recently but appear to have stopped, so there may be floating mines that we don't know about.'

Colonel Frolich stepped up and rolled out another larger scale plan of the area.

'Here is Nanjizal Bay, and this is the intended landing spot,' he pointed. 'If you look on this aerial colour photo you can see nearly the whole bay is strewn with underwater boulders and jagged rock outcrops. However, through here the clear turquoise colour indicates a narrow channel with sand on the sea bed. That's what you have to aim for,' he said, rather apologetically. 'It's not going to be easy. I suggest you study this photo very carefully to familiarise yourselves with the rocks that follow the line of the channel and the key landmarks on the cliff. There are caves at the back of the beach where you can stash the dinghy.'

'At the landing point you should use your flashlight to signal towards this point on the cliff edge, that's where your contact will be waiting. Make sure you cover the flashlight and point only at this spot. The cliffs are regularly patrolled. If there is no return signal you have to assume that it is not safe to move. Wait fifteen minutes and signal again. If there is no response then you proceed at your own discretion.'

'The cliffs here are not as precipitous as elsewhere around the bay but they are wet and slippery. This is a hand drawn sketch of the best route for you to follow. Here, and again here, your contact has secured ropes for you.'

'From the rendezvous point at the top of the cliff your contact will lead you on a safe path to bring you here, Boswednack Farm. This is your safe house. If you lose your contact, avoid the cliff path as it's regularly patrolled. Your best route is across either of these fields. Here is a sketch of the farmhouse. The yard is to the north and in the middle is a well. This is an important marker because the closest window, here, is the one you knock on. Three taps, pause, two taps, pause, and then one tap. A light will appear if it is safe, and you'll be let in.'

From the farm you are less than a mile from the Telegraph Station and you'll receive directions and advice from your contact. Is that clear, Dettsmann?'

'Yes, sir', he said. 'The ground intelligence is very good.'

'Yes it is,' replied Frolich. 'We have one of our best agents on the ground and he's your contact man – Agent Stiletto.'

'We leave on high tide at 07.20 am tomorrow. We'll rendezvous back in Nanjizal Bay at 23.00 hours on Monday 5 January,' said Thurmann.

'And if we don't make that rendezvous?' asked Dettsmann.

'There is no plan B. You'll be left to your own devices,' said Frolich.

Sunday 4 January 1942 – 4.15 pm

Destination Nanjizal Bay, Cornwall

U-553 had an eventful journey. In mid-channel an RAF Hudson had attacked them and they had to dive to the bottom, but at just two hundred and thirty feet, Thurmann would have liked to have been at least three hundred feet deeper. Dettsmann and his four troopers had not enjoyed the experience. The depth charges were too close for comfort as far as they were concerned, and the submarine had seemed to visibly twist and bend during the explosions. The crew seemed unperturbed and that made the troopers feel awkward.

'I'd rather attack a machine gun post across an open field,' whispered Herman Baecker who had tightly shaved blonde hair and the coldest of steel-blue eyes. His comrades nodded in agreement.

After the all-clear was sounded, U-553 resumed its journey northwest towards the southwest tip of Cornwall. The confrontation with the Hudson had delayed them an hour. This meant that instead of the plan to land at high tide in twilight it would now be an ebbing tide and almost dark.

'Up periscope,' said Thurmann, and he surveyed the shoreline and the black, brooding cliffs.

'Port twenty, slow ahead,' he barked.

Ten minutes later they were in position off the shoreline in Nanjizal Bay.

He ordered 'Surface, surface, surface,' and as the tanks were blown the U-boat broke surface three hundred yards from shore.

'Right', said Thurmann, 'let's go.'

Two sailors on the deck opened a hatch in the conning tower and pulled out a large bundle. They released it and as if by magic it hissed from a stowed bag to an inflated dinghy twelve feet long. Dettsmann and his four troopers passed their heavy backpacks and equipment into the dinghy and carefully climbed in. Rowing towards the shore, they had gone just fifty yards and when Dettsmann glanced back, U-553 had already disappeared from sight, leaving just a whirlpool of white water; he felt a shiver run down his spine.

Night was falling quickly and the small beach was not visible in the swell. They paddled fast and were one hundred yards offshore when they sighted waves swirling around submerged rocks directly in front of them.

'Left, left, left,' said Dettsmann and the two troopers on the right of the boat paddled frenetically.

The rubber dinghy slid over the edge of the rock, nearly tipping them up, but they kept their balance.

'Rocks ahead left,' said Dettsmann, and this time they had nowhere to go.

The swell dumped them right on top and the three troopers at the back of the dinghy were catapulted into the water. Miraculously, the dinghy slid over the rock and into calmer water. Dettsmann and Hanke shouted directions to the three troopers being swirled around in the skin-scraping eddies. Herman Baecker appeared by the dinghy and was pulled on board followed by Gert Fischer.

'Carl,' shouted Dettsmann, 'Carl, over here.'

One of the platoon shone a torch but Dettsmann ordered him to switch it off.

'We don't jeopardise the operation for anyone,' he reminded them.

They called and searched for another minute but there was no sign.

'OK paddle,' said Dettsmann in the building gloom.

He was cursing under his breath; the trooper would either be found by fishermen or washed up on the shore and spotted. They'd have to come back, search for and remove the evidence at first light.

They reached the boulder-strewn beach, offloaded their kit, deflated the boat, rolled it up and stashed it in one of the caves on the foreshore.

Dettsmann gave a dash-dot-dash signal with his torch and a light responded on the crest of the cliff towering above them. They redistributed the gear to incorporate Krueger's pack and weapons. Each pack was now over eighty pounds and they had to help one another lift and strap them on. There was no discernible path, just loose rubble and short, spiky gorse bushes that painfully brushed their cheeks as they worked up the cliff. At one point Dettsmann lost his footing and slid ten feet back down the cliff face only to be stopped by a sturdy thorn bush.

'God damn it,' he muttered.

Baecker threw him a short length of rope and he was able to pull himself out of his predicament. The climb took fifteen minutes, and when they cleared the crest of the cliff they knelt on one knee, gasping for breath. A light flashed and Dettsmann replied.

The Stranger approached and said in German, 'I'm Stiletto, welcome to Operation Cut-Throat.'

After catching their breath the four followed the Stranger across the cliff path into scrubland and headed in a south easterly direction.

They eventually arrived in the farm yard, and the Stranger indicated for them to wait by the well. The troopers gratefully eased their packs off and stretched with the relief. Although it was dark there was an air of decay about the place and it was clearly an abandoned farm although the farmhouse appeared large and sturdy. The house was in darkness as the Stranger walked to the back and knocked on the window. A faint light appeared and the back door opened and the Stranger beckoned the troopers to come in. As they entered the kitchen the warmth hit them and the smell of cooking food suddenly made them ravenous. A woman's scent added to the homeliness. It hadn't been like this in Smolensk, thought Hanke. A fire in the black Cornish range was visible and welcoming, particularly for Baecker and Fischer who were still soaked and distinctly uncomfortable in their wet, salt-laden clothes.

'Down here,' said the Stranger and led them down wooden steps leading from an open trapdoor.

'Welcome to your temporary home,' he said. 'Do not leave without the door being opened for you. You can signal your minder to let you out by pulling once on this rope. If there is no response, wait fifteen minutes before pulling again. There's water to wash, the latrine bucket, candles and matches. The transmitter is over there. The call sign is "Banjo", but only use it in an emergency and then for short duration – the British are monitoring all transmissions. I'll bring food and drink now. You two, give me your wet clothes and I'll get them washed and dried.'

He disappeared and the troopers heard a woman's voice in the distance.

'I wonder what else is on offer?' smirked Baecker.

Dettsmann glared at him; words were not necessary.

The Stranger reappeared with a large cast iron pot, a fresh loaf of bread and a kettle of hot coffee.

'Rabbit stew,' said the Stranger.

'By the way, we need to go back to Nanjizal Bay before first light,' said Dettsmann. 'We lost Carl and we need to—'

'Oh bloody hell,' said the Stranger, 'no, we can't risk you being seen, I'll have to go back, you rest and prepare. We go at 4 pm tomorrow. I'll be here at 2 pm for the final briefing.'

With that, he left and the trap door closed above them with a thud.

Sunday 4 January 1942 – 4.30 pm

Arrival in Plymouth Sound

Churchill was on the final leg of his return journey to England after his meetings with Roosevelt in Washington. The method and timing of his return had been contentious and hotly debated by his senior staff. HMS Duke of York and three escorts had been dispatched from the Clyde to pick up the Prime Minister in Bermuda. Sir Alistair Wilson, his Principal Private Secretary, had been apoplectic when he'd learned that Churchill was to fly back. A non-stop transatlantic flight was no small undertaking at this time even for a Boeing Clipper, widely regarded as representing the apex of flying boat technology.

Sir Alistair couldn't understand why he was not taking the safest option of going by sea. He called it tantamount to treason because all senior Government personnel knew Churchill was number one on the Nazis' assassination list. He swore that if anything happened to Churchill all senior military officers supporting this madness would be tried for treason.

Churchill, however, was pleased to have an option to get himself back to London five days faster, and a Boeing Clipper flying boat from the Royal Mail named 'Berwick' had been specially fitted out in order to carry enough fuel for the expected journey time of nearly twenty hours.

As Churchill quipped before he departed, 'If it manages to get over to Bermuda, it'll manage to get me back.'

Even so there was more than a little bravado in the decision; Churchill was the first world leader to attempt a non-stop trans-Atlantic flight. Staff in the Cabinet War Rooms said it was the first and only time Sir Alistair had been heard to use the f-word.

Taking off from Norfolk, Virginia, the previous morning the flight to Bermuda took just four hours. 'Berwick' was escorted by American fighter planes. Churchill had declined Roosevelt's offer but the President had insisted. He didn't want anything to happen to his friend and ally, particularly within American jurisdiction.

Departing Bermuda that morning with the weight of addi-

127

tional fuel for the twenty-hour flight back to Plymouth had proved challenging. 'Berwick' seemed to stick to the water and took twice the normal distance to lift off. It cleared the trees on the other side of the bay by just a hundred feet. Once airborne, Captain Rogers felt reassured that he had loaded enough fuel to land almost anywhere in the British Isles or Ireland. He needed that margin of error with the vagaries of the North Atlantic winds; whilst their destination was Plymouth they would only confirm that when they had established radio contact and received the weather for arrival.

Sixteen hours into the flight, Captain Rogers was informed that Churchill had had a good sleep and had finished breakfast. Hearing this, he went down the spiral staircase to the accommodation area and invited Churchill to the flight deck. When Churchill joined them, Rogers introduced the co-pilot, Bill George, and the navigator, Guy Jenkin.

'Mr Prime Minister, please sit here,' said George offering him the co-pilot's seat. Churchill nodded his gratitude, sat down and surveyed the horizon. White, cotton-like cumulus clouds passed below the plane and high cirrus cloud streamed above; the portent of an approaching weather front. At this altitude the winter sun was still strong enough to create bright beams of light radiating through the high cloud.

'My goodness, Rogers, I do envy the beautiful sights you experience in your job,' said Churchill. 'What a view you have from your office window.'

'Yes, Prime Minister, moments like this are very memorable and more than make up for the hours of routine. I remember one time flying into Hong Kong harbour, the sun shining through low mist and forming a circular rainbow. Absolutely beautiful. Mind you, it was a long way to go to see it!' he quipped. Churchill laughed and savoured the spectacle.

'How long until we land back in Blighty?'

'By my reckoning, Prime Minister, we're about two hours out,' said Rogers.

Pulling out a map, he pointed to a spot about three hundred miles south west of Lands End in Cornwall.

'We need to keep northwest of the Brest Peninsula here in Brittany because of the Jagdgeschwader fighter squadron. We'll overhead the Isles of Scilly up along the north coast of Cornwall and then cut across into Plymouth.

'Well, Rogers, you have a busy time coming up so I'll leave it to the professionals,' said Churchill. He saluted them and climbed down the staircase from the cockpit.

'Guy, give me an update on our position and an estimated time when we'll be within radio range of Plymouth Control. I'd like to know if we're cleared to land there or whether we need an alternate landing location,' said Rogers.

He stared out the window into the progressively thickening cloud and noted the wings were starting to ice on the leading edge.

Twenty minutes later Jenkin said, 'We should be within range now, captain.'

'Berwick to Plymouth Control, come in, over,' said Rogers, 'Berwick to Plymouth Control, come in, over.'

'Check we have the correct radio frequency, Bill. We should be able to speak with them by now,' he said to the co-pilot.

'Captain, let's drop below this cloud and we should get a sighting of the Scilly Isles any time now,' said Jenkin.

When they cleared the cloud base all three looked hopefully for the group of islands that would lead them onto Cornwall and their destination.

'That's bloody odd,' said George. 'There's just open sea, Guy ... double check, please. There's something wrong here.'

Looking straight ahead, Rogers squinted through the rain-streaked window. He couldn't believe what he saw.

'Guy, there's land ahead – is that Cornwall?' he asked.

'Negative, captain,' said George, 'We'd have radio contact if it was.'

'Captain, if the north westerly winds preceding this cold front have been stronger than we've adjusted for, we may have drifted south of our intended landfall,' said Jenkin.

'Shit, that means we're heading for Brittany,' Rogers said, and with that he swung the plane hard to port.

'Get a quick fix, Guy,' he said, 'and Bill, tune into the Luftwaffe frequency and see if we can expect company.'

'Captain, positive sighting, there's the Isle of Ushant. That puts us six miles south west of Brest,' said Jenkin. Rogers pulled the joy stick back to gain altitude and get back into the safety of the cloud.

'Captain my German is not good but they have detected something and they've scrambled some fighters. We have to assume they're for us,' said George.

'OK, let's maintain radio silence. We'll stay in this cloud and head northwest for fifteen minutes to get out of here, and then northeast to take us into Plymouth.'

Nearly fifteen minutes later Rogers said, 'Anything on the Luftwaffe frequency, Bill?'

'Negative, captain. Haven't heard anything for several minutes.'

'That's good. We'll turn now and keep radio silence for another ten minutes and then clear our arrival with Plymouth Control.'

'That's leaving it a bit late, isn't it, captain? We don't want to be mistaken for a German.' queried George.

'Well, Bill, if we break our silence too soon we'll be shot down by a Messerschmitt, and too late we'll be shot down by a Hurricane. Let me know when you think it's the right time,' said Rogers with a strained smile.

George glanced at the navigator and the captain but said nothing.

After the allotted ten minutes the captain tried the radio.

'Berwick to Plymouth Control, come in, over,' and this time the radio crackled into life.

'Plymouth Control receiving you, Berwick, over.'

'Plymouth Control this is Berwick ex Bermuda. Permission to land in Plymouth Sound, over.'

'Berwick, please confirm position, over.'

'Estimate thirty miles south of Plymouth, over.'

'Please repeat, Berwick, over.'

'Estimate thirty miles south of Plymouth, in cloud, zero visibility, over.'

'Standby, Berwick.'

'Plymouth Control to Berwick, we have you on radar, we wondered who you were, we've called off the hounds. Welcome back, confirm cargo on-board, over.'

'Plymouth Control, confirm cargo on-board, over.'

'That will be a relief to the whole nation, Berwick, well done, clear for your approach, over.'

'Start the approach, Bill. I'm just going to inform the Prime Minister,' said Rogers, beaming from ear to ear.

Monday 5 January 1942

Final preparations, Boswednack Farm

2.00 pm

The Stranger lifted the trap door in the kitchen at Boswednack Farm. He climbed down the steps and greeted Dettsmann and his team.

'OK, two hours and we go. You can move upstairs and stretch your legs and get your packs sorted. By the way, I looked for your man and there's no sign of him and it'll be dark in three hours so they won't find him until tomorrow at the earliest, and by then we'll be long gone,' said the Stranger. 'There's some bread, cold meats and soup on the kitchen table – help yourselves.'

Checking he wasn't being observed, the Stranger pulled out the radio, put the headphones on and selected the frequency. He looked at his watch and sat back and waited. At the allotted time the Morse code message from Berlin clicked in his headphones. The Stranger responded and wrote down the message, repeated it back, got confirmation and signed off. He pulled a small, soft, covered book from his pocket and set about deciphering the message. He reset the dial to a different frequency and tapped, 'banjo calling violin' and he waited. He tried again twice but there was no reply. He tried one last time and got the Morse code reply: 'violin receiving' came the message. He sent 'cutthroat go stop on time stop confirm pickup stop stay safe stop'.

He stashed the radio, climbed up the steps into the kitchen and beckoned Dettsmann over. He slipped him a piece of paper.

'Right,' he said, 'this is the message we have to send before we destroy the equipment. If I fail to send it, it'll be down to you. I'll tell you what to do?'

Dettsmann nodded.

'Let's go over the plan one last time,' said the Stranger, rolling out a map on the kitchen table.

'We leave the farm at 4 pm and rendezvous here at 5 pm,' he said pointing at the map, 'take our hostages and recheck watches. I enter here at 5.45 pm, open the security door at 6 pm here and let you in. We send the message at 6.10 pm, set explosives in the operations room at 6.20 pm and exit here. Because there will be a lot of military activity by this time, we'll head back separately and rendezvous here on Nanjizal beach at 10.15 pm. The first ones to arrive reinflate the dinghy. When we have all assembled we get loaded and then paddle out for the pick-up at 10.30 pm,' said the Stranger. 'Anyone not there at 10.20 pm gets left behind. If there are no questions, let's go over the detail. We need to time this perfectly.'

Monday 5 January 1942 – 2.00 pm
Naval Command, Devonport Dockyard

Colonel Bonham-Johns and Sir Alistair Wilson had flown down to RAF Roborough that morning and met Churchill for lunch in the Officers Mess at Naval Command Devonport. Sir Alistair was so relieved to see Churchill he'd shaken his hand warmly with both hands and wouldn't let go.

'Mr Churchill, we're so relieved you've arrived safely. You nearly gave us a heart attack yesterday. You approached Plymouth from an unexpected southerly direction and six Hurricanes from Fighter Command were scrambled to go and shoot you down,' said Sir Alistair, still shaking Churchill's hand.

Churchill was a little alarmed to hear this, but said nonchalantly, 'well, Alistair, fortunately they failed in their mission, and let's just say the weather was on our side. Now then, Julian, give me an update before the meeting.'

'Well, sir, Hotspur and Prince of Wales docked safely two days ago and are being repaired and replenished. Captain Edwin Rabjohn from Hotspur and Captain George Ashwood from the Prince of Wales will be with us at 3 pm for the meeting. Admiral Maxwell has joined us at your request, and Rear Admiral Thornton has just arrived – he was diverted by bad weather and had to land in Belfast on the way down. He's freshening up as we speak. He'll be able to update us on the current status of USS Washington and USS Wichita, but they should be approaching Scapa Flow. So we have the northern North Sea covered and the Western Approaches covered, sir.'

'That's good, my boy,' said Churchill, 'but I also have some good news to tell the meeting – Tuscaloosa is on her way to assist. When I spoke with the President, he was initially adamant that the USA's priority was to fight the Japanese in the Pacific. But as chance would have it, the day we spoke, U-boats attacked shipping off of Long Island and then at other locations along their Eastern Seaboard. Nothing could have provided a more salutary warning of the threat that the Axis presents right across the Atlantic. The audacity of Donitz to attack with such force three thousand miles from base was a shock to the Americans. So you see, where I had failed to persuade them the Nazis succeeded,' said Churchill with a conciliatory smile.

'The thing that the President was most concerned about was the US Navy's apparent inability to send secure messages. He described it as "being like a leaky megaphone". So having agreed to send the three ships we requested he only communicated two, Washington and Wichita. We agreed that Tuscaloosa would sail two days later, supposedly in support of a convoy. But not a word of this, Julian, I want to notify her involvement at the appropriate time during the meeting, right my boy?'

'Yes, sir, absolutely,' said Bonham-Johns with a broad grin and thinking, you wily old bulldog you did pull a rabbit out of the hat after all.

Bonham-Johns looked at his watch and said, 'It's time for our meeting, sir. Thank you for the heads-up.'

They entered the drab utilitarian meeting room lit only by overhead electric lights. For security reasons the room chosen was in the basement of Naval Head Quarters. Bonham-Johns introduced Captain George Ashwood from the Prince of Wales and Captain Edwin Rabjohn from Hotspur, and they saluted and shook hands warmly.

'So I believe congratulations are in order, Captain Rabjohn. I understand you sank U-79 and three Italian cruisers off Tobruk last month – a real high-point in our gruelling battle with the Axis forces in the Mediterranean. Well done.'

Rabjohn nodded in recognition of the compliment.

'And Rear Admiral Thornton, did you have a good flight?'

Thornton had dark circles around his eyes and looked pallid. He didn't appear to be at all well.

'It was a long flight, Mr Prime Minister, and a little bumpy, but much to be expected at this time of year,' he said, tensing the muscles in his right leg to stop it shaking.

'Quite so,' said Churchill, 'I flew in from Bermuda yesterday – actually the bad weather was something of a saviour in my case.'

Thornton stared at Churchill and wondered if he was being sarcastic.

'Right, gentlemen, to business,' said Churchill.

As they took their allotted seats, Thornton, already uncomfortable, grimaced at being addressed as a gentleman again, but did not seek eye contact.

'Please give us an update, Julian.'

'Thank you, Prime Minister. Tirpitz's commissioning is now a matter of a day or two away. Our agent in Wilhelmshaven will notify us when she sails. We have HMS Hotspur and HMS Prince of Wales here in Devonport being repaired and replenished and they will sail east up the English Channel destined for Portsmouth, escorted by HMS Faulknor and one submarine. Sailing time will be finalised in the next 24 hours. We will make sure the Germans know where they are so that Tirpitz doesn't try and bolt for the Atlantic. When she sails for Norway they will follow her up the North Sea. In the north we have Washington and Wichita, and can I ask you the status please, Rear Admiral?' said Bonham-Johns.

'Thank you, colonel,' said Thornton. 'Both anchored in Scapa Flow this morning and are being replenished. They were engaged by U-boats and two light cruisers off the northwest coast of Scotland but received only minor damage. They'll be ready for action within 24 hours.' He looked rather pleased with himself.

'That is good news, sir,' said Bonham-Johns.

'Right, here are the written orders for Operation Harpoon with our ranking of the highest probability for Tirpitz's movements in section 2a. I will refer to the admiralty chart of the North Sea at the back of that section. I have also included two alternative strategies listed as 2b and 2c.'

'When Tirpitz has sailed we'll communicate to the fleet with the code word 'Gauntlet'. Washington and Wichita will patrol the area between Scapa Flow in the Orkney Isles and the Shetland Isles to stop her entering the North Atlantic. They will be supported by destroyers Firedrake, Foresight and Escapade and two submarines. That will force Tirpitz to keep close to the Norwegian coast, but if she tries to make a break for it the orders are to engage her. We are, however, quite confident she will head into Trondheim fjord. All our intelligence indicates that she will refuel at one of two recently constructed locations. When we get word that she's sailed from Wilhelmshaven, RAF Coastal Command from Lossiemouth will attack the newly constructed fuel store at Beitstadfjord. That will leave the Germans with the one remaining option of refuelling at Fættenfjord. This is the more exposed of the two sites and offers the highest chance of success in damaging Tirpitz whilst she's docked. We'll close the trap with Washington and Wichita standing offshore to the North and Hotspur and Prince of Wales to the south. Whilst Tirpitz is being refuelled, we plan a large scale bombing raid. We'll drop five-ton "Tallboy" bombs and sea mines. If the weather is against us we'll have our eight ships and three submarines waiting to engage her.'

'So Julian, the million-dollar question: when does Tirpitz sail?' asked Churchill.

'And what makes you think she won't turn east into the Baltic Sea to undergo sea trials?' added Thornton.

Bonham-Johns took a few seconds to collect his thoughts.

'Well, both are critical questions, of course, and I wish we had a definitive answer. As to timing, we believe she's all but ready and they'll sail probably in the next bad weather. The Met boys say the next weather front will come through tomorrow night so it could be as soon as that. As to your question, Rear Admiral, will she go east rather than north? The Baltic is an option but there is no direct military activity there. She could potentially disrupt any supplies bound for Leningrad and indeed she could shell the city. But there are few supplies getting in by that route, and it would be a waste of Tirpitz's capabilities. We believe she's actually most needed in their Mediterranean campaign but that means she'd have to run the gauntlet down the English Channel, and we don't think the Führer will risk his new toy doing that. That leaves escape to the north as the most probable option. The Germans occupy Norway, so have support and logistics capabilities right up to the Arctic Circle. The Arctic Convoys are supporting their arch enemy Russia, and once she's up there she also creates options to sail south around the west of Britain to the Med, or north to Iceland itself. We know the Nazis have their eye on invading Iceland, so maybe that's their next military target?'

Thornton's brow furrowed. He hadn't considered that.

'Thank, you, Julian. Well, gentlemen, that's the status and the plan,' said Churchill. 'I do, however, have one additional bit of information that is material to our plan that you need to know about. When I met with the President two weeks ago he generously agreed to release three war ships.'

He paused and looked around the room.

'Gentlemen, the Germans are a smart and intelligent enemy. They intercept our transatlantic communications, they broke the US Navy Hagelin code more than twelve months ago and have enemy agents in all the major naval ports on the Eastern Seaboard of the United States, and they have at least two in Hvalfjörður.' Churchill again paused for effect.

'For that reason the President and I agreed to communicate that only Washington and Wichita would join Operation Harpoon. We did not communicate that USS Tuscaloosa would follow two days later, ostensibly as an escort for a convoy to Liverpool. She has split from the convoy off the west coast of Ireland and is headed around the north of Scotland to dock in Sullom Voe in the Shetland Isles on the 8th. That means we have two battleships, three heavy cruisers, three destroyers and three submarines in the right place at the right time. In addition, we have air cover from RAF Lossiemouth. Gentlemen, with those odds the plan is to attack Tirpitz and her three escorts before she gets to Trondheim. Julian, you work with Rear Admiral Thornton and Admiral Maxwell to modify the battle plan,' said Churchill.

Admiral Maxwell said, 'Prime Minister, why would we risk five of our biggest assets in the Atlantic when as Julian says we can use them to intimidate Tirpitz into Trondheim? If the RAF can immobilise or destroy her in dock we can use the eight ships to good effect elsewhere.'

'Admiral, Tirpitz is a new ship with a new crew and they are unlikely to be fully battle-ready,' said Churchill.

'Yes, but her three escorts certainly are, and I don't need to tell you how precious our naval fleet is in case of Nazi attack across the Channel,' said Maxwell.

'Admiral, it may be some time before such an opportunity arises again. We will engage her in the North Sea and if she escapes into Trondheim we still have the RAF option,' said Churchill, 'modify the plan.'

The meeting was interrupted by a loud and insistent knock on the door.

'Sir, apologies for the intrusion but there's an urgent call for Colonel Bonham-Johns.'

Bonham-Johns gave his apology and followed the Officer to a private room with a single red phone on a desk.

'Just press the white button, sir,' he said, and shut the door behind him.

Bonham-Johns picked up the receiver and pressed the button.

'Hello, Bonham-Johns.'

'Ah Julian, its Cliff here. I'm so glad I caught you. We picked up a transmission at 2.15 this afternoon from Abwehr to Agent Banjo. The message is of course coded and the boffins will take a few hours to work it out. The crucial thing is that it was a longer message than normal, and it appears Banjo repeated it back. We've managed to get a good fix – it's definitely west of Penzance.'

'West of Penzance?' quizzed Bonham-Johns. 'So what target is there in that area that will help Tirpitz and Operation Cut-Throat? I was sure it must be Devonport but clearly not. Anyway, good work, Cliff. I don't need to tell you we must get that message deciphered pronto. Make sure they know it's priority one. Nothing else matters. I need to get down to west Cornwall and find out what's happening. And let me know immediately if you get anything, no matter how small. You can always get me via the Prime Minister,' he added.

When he returned to the meeting, Bonham-Johns was elated.

'Well, Mr Churchill, we now know Agent Stiletto's target is the far west of Cornwall, in fact west of Penzance. It has to be the radar installations at RAF Portreath or RAF Sennen or the Porthcurno Telegraph Station. They're all high security areas so it's difficult to know what they might be up to. Sir, with your permission I need to fly down to RAF Sennen immediately to take stock. Hopefully this will put us one jump ahead.'

'Agreed, my boy, and take my security man, Captain Hunt. He'll be in the officers' mess. I don't want you coming to any harm.'

'Gentlemen, excuse me whilst I make arrangements for the colonel. Work on our revised plan for Operation Harpoon. I want to review it within the hour,' said Churchill, and with that they left.

Within minutes, Bonham-Johns and Hunt were speeding out of the Dockyard gates, heading the five miles out of town to RAF Roborough.

'Sir,' said the sailor who was driving, 'the air raid sirens have just started – I have to turn back.'

'No, sailor, put your foot down, for God's sake, and get us to Roborough as quick as you can.'

'Aye, aye, sir,' he replied, very much against his better judgement.

It took them twenty minutes to get to the airfield, and Bonham-Johns was relieved to see they were expected as the gates were immediately opened and they were waved through. The Boss has done it again, he thought.

The car was directed straight to a waiting Mosquito.

'Sir, I'm sorry – we can't leave now, there's an air raid just started,' said the Flight Lieutenant.

'We've got to go now,' said Bonham-Johns. 'It's a matter of national security.'

'Alright, sir, but I just need to make you aware the bombers have escort fighters, and our Hurricanes have just gone up after them as well. Either side might mistake us for the other,' he added.

'Flight, I don't care. We've got to go – now – is that clear? Anyway, it's probably a good time to slip away with all this action. Let's go.'

They all scrambled through the belly door, and Bonham-Johns sat in the co-pilot's seat. He wasn't going to miss out on this experience. Hunt squeezed into what was usually the bomb bay.

'Remember this isn't a bloody bombing mission,' Hunt shouted at the Flight.

The plane quickly taxied to the end of the runway amidst the racket of anti-aircraft guns. As the plane picked up speed on the runway the first flashes from the bombing raid flickered behind them. The pilot's comment about not wanting to be mistaken for the enemy took on a new poignancy. As the plane climbed up through the cloud the flashes from the bombing took on a ghostly aura. Bonham-Johns had never experienced anything like it before.

'You alright back there, captain?' yelled Bonham-Johns, and he got a thumbs-up from Hunt.

When the Mosquito broke through the top of the cloud the pilot had to take immediate evasive action, flinging the joy stick violently to starboard to avoid a Heinkel 111 bomber that flashed by, less than one hundred feet to their left. Bonham-Johns clearly saw the pilot's face lit by the instrument panel. Jesus Christ, that was a close one, he thought. The pilot immediately dived back into the clouds to avoid being shot at and took a wide berth around the bomber formation. They had avoided a collision by just a split second.

'What was that?' Hunt shouted from the back.

'You don't want to know,' shouted Bonham-Johns, smiling.

Staring out into the blackness, Bonham-Johns could see nothing but flashes of light, which fortunately were getting fainter.

'How do you avoid a collision in cloud at night?' Bonham-Johns finally asked.

'Oh, by sheer pilot skill, sir,' he said, 'and a large dose of good luck and providence.'

Bonham-Johns just caught the smile, lit by the dim instrument lights.

After twenty minutes the Flight spoke on the radio and then climbed above the cloud and switched his navigation lights on.

'Don't want to be mistaken for the enemy after all that, do we?' he quipped. 'Landing in twenty minutes, colonel. It'll be a hard landing as the runway is very short. It is designed to take only small planes that bring the daily mail bags from London to Porthcurno Telegraph,' said the Flight in a casual, matter-of-fact way.

—— ᘓᘔ ——

Monday 5 January 1942 – 4.00 pm

Raid on Security Area 28, Porthcurno

4.05 pm

Dettsmann crouched behind the hedge and shone a small torch on the map and checked their position. The platoon fell in behind him.

'We follow this hedge for eighty yards, and there's a thickly wooded stream beyond that, which takes us down to St Levan,' he whispered.

He signalled to his team to follow. They set off at a fast pace even though their packs were heavy, containing explosives, detonators, rope and climbing equipment. Each carried a Sauer semi-automatic pistol in a holster, spare ammunition, an MP 40 submachine gun and hand grenades. They were supremely fit, and this was second nature to them.

The scrubland was a mass of gorse and bramble bushes; very dense and eight feet high. As they disappeared into the thicket, the needle-sharp leaves and thorns scratched their exposed skin and drew blood.

'Damn and blast these bloody bushes,' muttered Dettsmann as he forged on. Breaking cover, the platoon dropped to one knee on his signal. He referred to the map again, pointed, and they entered the valley wood. After ten minutes' stumbling through the dark, uneven and boggy terrain they came to the field. Stopping and referring to the map one last time, he pointed to the track that would take them down to St Levan.

'We'll keep to this side of the hedge and we'll end up close to the Porthcurno road,' said Dettsmann.

As they moved forward, a dog barked nearby and they fell into the hedge in near silence. Knives were slid silently from their sheaths. The dog barked again, closer this time.

'Wassup, Bob, you smelled a rabbit?' said a man.

He was on the track the other side of the hedge; just ten feet away. The dog appeared on the hedge right above the troopers and went berserk, barking and snarling. The Germans didn't move a muscle.

'Come 'ere, you silly bugger, you'll scare the rabbits,' yelled the man.

But the dog didn't obey and jumped from the hedge right in front of the Germans. As the dog landed it snarled showing its teeth.

'What the 'ell you on about Bob, come 'ere you silly bugger,' shouted the man from the other side of the hedge.

The dog went for Herman Baecker and grabbed a jaw-full of clothing, wrenching from side to side. The German raised his machine gun and hit it over the head, but it was a glancing blow and the dog yelped loudly and leapt back, struggling to stand up.

'Wassup, you silly bugger? Come 'ere, Bob,' said the man. The dog obeyed this time and scrambled, less nimbly, up the hedge and disappeared.

The man said, 'come 'ere you silly bugger, what the ... ?' The man felt a flap of skin and warm blood streaming from the dog's head. 'Shit,' he said, and ran off down the track with the dog lumbering dazed behind him.

'We've got to stop him before he reports this,' said Dettsmann. 'Gert quick, you go, if you're not back in three minutes we'll move on to the first rendezvous.'

Sliding out of his backpack, Gert Fischer was over the hedge and on the chase in seconds. It was dark in the lane, and the uneven and muddy surface was not easy to run on. He slipped twice; the second time he cracked his knee hard on a rock and was slowed down. Within a short distance the lane opened into a yard with farm outbuildings on two sides, and he stopped and massaged his knee and held his breath, listening intently. Seconds passed and he heard nothing. He walked on cautiously and then behind and to his right he heard a faint whimper. He walked on a few steps and then dropped down and moved right into any empty building. He listened ... but nothing. Where the hell are you? he thought. He retraced his steps and then heard the whimper again. Knife in hand, he hugged the wall and glanced around. He could just make out the dog lying on the ground. It growled weakly. He needed to silence it and stepped forward, knife still in his hand. He bent over and slit its throat, and the dog gurgled and twitched. As Gert Fischer stood up, pain shot though his back, his lungs burst, his legs lost feeling and he collapsed, head spinning and whirring, and then a wave of blackness.

Harry Nancarrow stood over the body, holding a heavy Cornish shovel.

He flicked his lighter and checked the dog. 'Oh shit,' he said, 'you poor old thing, Bob.' The dog was dead.

He then turned to the prostrate figure.

'So who the 'ell are you mate and why'd you kill my dog?' he said with anger, and held the flame close to the prone body.

'Oh my God, it's a bloody Kraut soldier, oh dear Lord, oh Jesus protect us.'

His mind was in a frenzy. He could see blood pouring from the German's nose, and his eyes stared unblinking.

'Oh sweet Jesus, I've killed him, what the 'ell do I do?' he thought. 'Got to warn Bert, yes that's it, got to warn Bert.'

'Sorry Bob, old boy, I'm so sorry, I'll come back for you,' he said as he turned and ran down the hill towards Porthcurno and Boscarn Hamlets.

4.25 pm

The Stranger stood behind bushes on the opposite side of the road to Boscarn Hamlets. He waited patiently in the shadows, watching house number three carefully. Five minutes to go before the scheduled departure. At 4.30 there was no sign of the old man. Five minutes, then six minutes past and still no sign.

'Silly old fool, where the hell are you?' he muttered, 'why tonight?'

At 4.38, Bert Chenoweth finally appeared and closed the front door behind him. He was dressed against the cold in his Home Guard trench coat, balaclava and tin hat, rifle slung over his shoulder. A rasping cough stopped him in his tracks for a few moments, and he then walked briskly down the hill towards the village hall.

When Bert was out of sight the Stranger emerged from the

shadows and walked towards the row of cottages. He moved with pace but tried not to appear in a hurry. In fact he was. He'd lost nearly ten valuable minutes and was going to miss his man at this rate. He opened the small garden gate and walked brazenly up to the door of number three, looked around, and knocked. After a few moments Clara opened the door, wiping her wet hands on a tea towel. She looked at the Stranger and immediately recognised him, and was about to greet the man, but a cloth was forced over her mouth, with a knife at her throat. She held her breath and stared into the cold, steely eyes. Alarmed, she had to take a breath and the sweet, sickly ether entered her lungs and, with her head spinning, she slipped to the floor. I wish I'd given you that on the bus, the Stranger thought.

Closing and bolting the front door he moved down the hall and put his ear to the kitchen door. He could hear talking inside. Taking the Webley pistol from his coat pocket, he barged the door open and entered. Megan gave a muffled scream putting her hand to her mouth and Robert was about to challenge him but saw the gun.

'Now, do as I say and no one gets hurt,' said the Stranger.

Robert's mind was racing.

'Face down on the floor,' he said to Robert, 'now, if you don't want any harm to come to your family.'

The baby started to cry, and Megan looked pleadingly at the Stranger. He nodded at her and she picked the baby out of the cot and held her tight.

Robert hadn't moved. He was trying to work out what to do. The Stranger raised his gun to pistol-whip him and, seeing it was useless, knelt on the floor.

'I said face down on the floor,' snapped the Stranger. 'If you don't do as I say, I will hurt you. Now, hands behind your back.'

Dropping on one knee, he pulled leather loops from his belt and quickly tied Roberts's wrists. Little do you know, reflected the Stranger, I need you alive.

Grabbing him by the collar, he lifted him up and dumped him in the tall-back chair by the Cornish range.

'What have you done with Mother?' said Robert. 'If you've hurt her I'll—'

He looked into the Stranger's cold eyes and dried up.

'I've shut her up. It's about time someone did, and I'll do the same with her if you don't do what I say,' he said, pointing at Megan.

Robert couldn't swallow and was breathing heavily; he'd never felt so scared and helpless.

'You,' the Stranger said to Megan, 'sit there.' He pointed with his gun and used more leather loops to tie her legs to the chair. He glanced out into the hall to ensure Clara was still unconscious.

'Right,' he said to Robert, 'let me tell you what we're going to do.'

4.50 pm

Nearly an hour after the German troops had departed, Eleanor Bannencourt had cleared the farmhouse of all personal effects and evidence of their presence. She burned documents, codes, maps and clothes and packed a small leather rucksack with a few personal effects and the detailed report and maps of the area compiled by the Stranger. Last of all, she packed the biscuit tin sized parcel that she'd received from London two days before.

After hiding the rucksack she left the farmhouse and walked east across the fields towards Porthcurno. She kept to the hedges as far as possible to avoid being seen and when she got to her vantage point above the Telegraph Station she settled down and waited for the action.

4.50 pm

Dettsmann and the two remaining troopers, Baecker and Hanke, crossed Porthcurno road, went through the gate and carefully circled behind Boscarn Hamlets looking specifically for number three. On Dettsmann's signal, Hanke gave an owl hoot and seconds later the back door opened and Dettsmann and Baecker slipped in. Hanke remained in the garden, keeping watch.

'There's one in the corridor. Bring her in and tie her up,' said the Stranger. Baecker unceremoniously dragged her in by the feet, picked her up and dropped her in Bert's chair by the Cornish Range; he tied her right wrist to the arm of the chair. She started to stir, opened her eyes and stared at the surroundings. She wanted to scream, to tell them to leave her family alone, but her body wouldn't work. She couldn't speak; the only sound she made was a weak groan.

'I'm going on down to the Telegraph with young Robert here, and remember, be at the escape shaft in forty-five minutes,' said the Stranger in German.

'Check watches ... 5.15 in five, four, three, two, one, now. They clicked their watches is unison.

Ramming his stiletto knife into Robert's ribs he said, 'Now you do exactly as I say and your family won't get hurt.'

He cut the leather tie, allowing Robert to put his coat on.

'Don't forget your lunch bag,' he said, and they left by the front door, Baecker locking it behind them.

Dettsmann looked at his blond trooper.

'Ten minutes, Herman, wait ten minutes. Then kill them and meet me at the escape shaft. Remember the signal – I don't want to shoot you by mistake.' With that, he let himself out the back door. The trooper smiled and leered at Megan. He was going to enjoy this.

5.25 pm

The Stranger walked down the road with Robert half a pace ahead on his right-hand side. Robert's legs were unsteady and he walked like a marionette; he had to consciously put each foot forward in turn. How the hell did this happen, why me, why my family? he thought. Tears ran down his cheek; he was in a complete panic. He thought of Megan, baby May and his Mother at home.

'Do exactly as I say or they all die, and it won't be pretty,' the Stranger said. 'If you don't do exactly what I say it'll be a slow and painful end, little slices removed, a piece at a time. The baby first, then your mother and then your wife.'

'You never know, Herman might just have a bit of fun before the final act,' hissed the Stranger right in Robert's ear.

Robert felt the bile rise in his stomach, he wanted to be sick, and he thought he was going to collapse. The Stranger's knife dug in his ribs and refocused his attention.

'Ow do I know you won't just kill 'em anyway?' Robert said.

'You'll just have to trust me, won't you?' said the Stranger, 'we have nothing to gain from killing them, provided you behave. Your obedience is all I require, and I will get it,' he added, digging the stiletto into his ribs to emphasise the point.

As they approached the first checkpoint, they passed two soldiers wheeling a large ammunition box towards the building marked Bus Stop. As they got close, the door opened and the machine gun emplacement inside was clearly visible.

Shit, thought the Stranger, that's an unexpected turn-up, and his mind raced as to the implications. It's OK, he thought, the plan was to access the Telegraph by the escape shaft, so they'd keep well away from this little viper's nest.

At the checkpoint, both Robert and the Stranger showed their passes.

The guard flashed his light in the Stranger's face and said, 'You're new aren't you, mate?'

'Yes, I'm just down from London, arrived yesterday.'

The light flashed to Robert.

'You alright, mate?' he asked. 'You don't look so good.'

'Touch of the gip,' Robert replied.

'OK, go on through,' said the guard.

They passed the second checkpoint with similar questions and waited outside the huge metal door that was access point A. The loud Klaxon horn sounded and the guard slowly pulled the door open.

It suddenly dawned on Robert.

'You fuckin bastard,' he said, 'you got that pass from Josh Tregembo didn't you. What the 'ell did you do with him, you bastard?'

A sense of dread washed over Robert.

'The same as we'll do to your family if you don't do exactly what I say.'

'Oh dear God, we're all going to die, I'll never see my family again,' mumbled Robert.

The stiletto was jabbed hard into his ribs and Robert said, 'Go on, you bastard, why don't you kill me now?'

The Stranger twisted his arm and pressed the knife harder. 'Remember your family, and if you want them to live, do exactly as I say. Now move.'

Robert's legs wobbled and the Stranger literally frogmarched him into the reception area and the door banged shut behind them. When the inner door opened, they acknowledged the duty Sergeant and walked down the long, whitewashed concrete corridor deep into the hill.

5.25 pm

Harry Nancarrow stumbled down the steep road from St Levan, his legs hardly able to carry him. His lungs were burning, his heart thumping out of his chest. He turned left, struggled the half-mile up the road and collapsed against the door of number three.

He banged it hard. 'Bert,' he yelled, 'are you there, Bert?'

He banged and banged. 'Bert, Bert.'

Inside, Herman Baecker was alarmed. He checked Megan's leather ties and said in broken English, 'Any trouble, I slit baby, then you.'

Megan stared at him in horror and nodded her head.

Clara was coming around and stared at the trooper. Her head was thumping painfully and her buttock was hurting again after her fall in the hall. She was wracking her brains on what to do but couldn't focus.

The trooper went to the front door that was visibly shaking. Got to stop this, he thought, the whole village will be alerted at this rate. He slid the bolt, turned the key and quickly opened the door, grabbed the man and pulled him in. He head-butted him hard in the face, and the man went down like a sack of potatoes. Not even looking outside, he locked and bolted the door and walked back into the kitchen. He looked around; they were all in place. What he hadn't seen was the vegetable knife in Clara's hand; the one that she had been using to peel potatoes and had dropped in the pocket on the front of her apron when the

Stranger had called. He went back into the hall and tied and gagged the latest visitor.

Clara was frenetically trying to cut the rope tying her right wrist. Her arthritic hand ached and her head thumped terribly, but she kept trying.

Herman came back into the kitchen dragging the semi-conscious man who had blood streaming from his nose and a huge and growing purple lump in the centre of his forehead.

'Oh my God, Harry, you alright?' Clara exclaimed. 'What have you done to Harry, you bugger?'

Harry groaned.

Oh my God, she thought, I've got to work quickly. She caught Megan's eye and nodded at the baby. Megan looked back quizzically. What does Mother mean? she wondered.

Clara wrinkled her face. Oh God no, Megan thought, but she'd seen Clara cutting the rope and knew it was their only chance; she had to create a diversion for all their sakes.

The baby was asleep on her lap when she pinched her on the leg. Straight away the baby bawled, then took a deep breath and with a quivering bottom lip she cried and cried.

The trooper was not amused and told her to, 'shut up or I slit,' waving his knife at her.

But the baby didn't stop and the trooper got more and more agitated. He moved towards Megan and pressed the knife against the baby and Megan screamed in terror. He then put the knife against Megan's cheek and started to run it down towards her neck. He cut the front of her dress, exposing her underwear, and eyed her ample cleavage. Clara was cutting at the leather ties like a person possessed when Herman glanced back and saw what she was doing. He quickly turned from Megan and stabbed Clara in the arm, and the vegetable knife dropped to the flagstone floor with a clatter.

With a wild, vindictive expression, he grabbed Clara by the hair and brought the knife to her cheek. He pressed it slowly and deliberately deep into the flesh and started to cut down towards her throat. The pain was intense and Clara tightened every muscle in her body; she knew she was going to die. She felt a wave hit her, her ears started to ring, she part-opened her eyes and all she could see was red, and her face felt suddenly hot and tingly; her mind was swirling, she felt as though she were in free fall, and then slipped into darkness. Megan screamed uncontrollably at the top of her voice and couldn't look at her Mother. She stared at the floor and the prostrate trooper; he had half his head missing – it had just exploded all over the kitchen.

At that moment the back door was kicked open and Bert stormed in.

'Oh my God, you alright Megan?' he said, but she just continued to scream and shake uncontrollably.

May was screaming as well. He looked at Clara, slumped in the chair with her head bent back, covered in blood, bits of bone and brain with a large slash down her right cheek.

'Oh God,' he thought, 'the bastard's killed her.'

Harry Nancarrow was semi-conscious on the floor, his face covered in blood.

He looked down and dark red blood puddled around the head of the trooper who lay dead on the flagstones. It was like a scene from Armageddon. Bert started getting flashbacks to the trenches in the Somme where 23 years earlier he'd killed his last of many Germans.

5.35 pm

Eleanor Bannencourt heard the single shot ring out, and it echoed back and forth across the valley. Using her torch she checked her watch. That's twenty-five minutes early she thought. Was it part of the raid or something else? She wasn't sure and became anxious. She looked over the hedge into the valley but didn't see anything untoward. She settled back again and waited nervously.

5.35 pm

Dettsmann and Niklas Hanke were working their way up the hillside above the Telegraph Station when they also heard the single shot. They stopped and listened but there was no further shooting so they continued along the track to the large sandbagged emplacement and dropped to the ground. Dettsmann signalled for Hanke to wait and crawled forward. When he got to the sand bag wall he stopped and listened. Dropping his pack and machine gun he drew his knife and put it between his teeth and slid silently over the wall. He slithered like a snake on the hunt. One muffled cry was the only noise.

He signalled for Hanke to join him. In the middle of the bunker two soldiers lay dead, their throats cut. Hiding under the tarpaulin, they had been playing cards by a small oil lamp. They had been completely unaware of Dettsmann's arrival.

In the centre of the emplacement was a concrete structure with a small but heavy steel door set in the north side. It was constructed of two-inch diameter iron bars and appeared impenetrable. Warm, moist, metallic-smelling air vented from the door. Dettsmann shone his light inside. A flight of steep steps ran down into the darkness. It was impossible to see where it led. He looked at his watch: 5.46. The remaining fourteen minutes seemed an interminable prospect.

5.35 pm
Inside the Telegraph Station the Stranger, holding tight onto Robert, skirted around the instrument room and made directly for the security office.

The Stranger knocked on the door.

'Come in,' said a voice inside.

With that the Stranger pushed Robert forward and followed him in.

'Hello, Robert,' said Jeff Atkinson, the head of security, 'are you alright?'

With that the Stranger appeared and grabbed Robert by the neck and held the stiletto to his throat.

'Do exactly as I say,' said the Stranger, 'or this one gets three inches of steel in the neck and then it'll be your turn. Move away from the desk and don't try and hit the panic alarm. If you do I'll slit his throat and then take great delight in slitting yours.'

'Now back away and get the keys for the escape door.'

'Don't do it, Jeff,' said Robert, with deeply misplaced bravado. With that the Stranger stuck the stiletto in Robert's cheek with a slow, deliberate movement and slit it open. He screeched with pain. Blood ran down his neck and soaked into his shirt collar. The security man's thoughts of resistance immediately subsided and he knelt down to open the safe where the key was kept.

5.38 pm
Bert wasted no time in cutting Clara, Megan and Harry free and then applied first aid to Clara. He got a tea towel and soaked it in cold water and started to wipe her face clean. Her arm was bleeding profusely where she'd been stabbed. The cold on her face started to bring her round, and she looked mesmerized, staring into Bert's face.

'Bert,' she blurted out, 'what the—?'

'Shhh, don't talk, Clara. You're alright, you're all alright,' he said reassuringly.

She had a serious gash on her cheek and neck but it didn't look life threatening. Clara stared in astonishment at the trooper lying on the floor.

'Dear God what the 'ell happened?' she asked.

'I saw Harry here running down the road shouting for me but I couldn't get his attention. When he banged on our door and was dragged inside I knew there was trouble, so I came around the back and looked in the kitchen window, and when he pointed his knife at you I shot him.'

'No wonder he's such a mess,' spluttered Harry. 'Shooting him at close range with a Lee-Enfield – his head just exploded, Bert. I never seen nothin' like it ... and I laid out another German soldier up above St Levan, I hit him with a shovel, I think I killed 'im an' all.'

'Oh God', exclaimed Clara, 'I just remembered, he's got Robert.'

'Who's got Robert, what do you mean?' asked Bert.

'The man I met ... he's got Robert, they've gone down to the Telegraph and a German captain is out there somewhere as well, oh Bert if anything happens to that boy how will I ever tell Ross his boy's gone?' and with that she burst into tears.

'That's not going to happen,' he said. 'Who is this man? I don't understand.'

'I met him on the Penzance bus when I went shoppin' before Christmas. He's one of us ... I mean, he's English or ... oh I don't know, perhaps a bit foreign. He's got a gash on his forehead from the bombing of the railway station.'

'Why did Robert go with him to the Telegraph?' he asked, not understanding.

'He was kidnapped,' blurted Megan. 'The Stanger forced him at knifepoint.'

'Shit, I've got to warn the station,' Bert said, and looked around for his rifle but then thought of a better alternative. Kneeling over the dead trooper, he pulled the Sauer pistol from the holster. This'll get some attention, he thought. He went out into the back garden but wasn't familiar with the model and it took a few seconds to arm. He pointed the gun in the air and fired off the entire magazine. The noise of the shots echoed all around the valley.

5.50 pm

Dettsmann and Hanke clearly heard the shots.

'That's a Sauer – it must be Herman,' said Dettsmann.

'Or Gert?' suggested Hanke.

Dettsmann wracked his brains as to why either would fire off a whole magazine with no return shots. He glanced at his watch: 5.50. Where the hell are they, he wondered and shone his torch down the steps again. No one; where the bloody hell are they?

A radio crackled under the tarpaulin: 'Come in post five, come in. Come in Jim, come in, we heard shooting, are you OK?' said a rather concerned voice.

'Oh shit', said Dettsmann, 'there's got to be a change of plan, we have to assume this place will be crawling with soldiers in minutes. This is what we're going to do, Hanke. We'll have to blow the door from the top. Use most of the explosives and put it here, here and here. We'll just have to improvise when we're inside.'

'Come in, post five, come in, Jim come in,' said the concerned voice on the radio.

5.50 pm

The volley of shots made Eleanor Bannencourt jump. She recognised the sound of the Sauer. Although it was still early it was clear the raid had started. Minutes later a huge explosion on the hill opposite confirmed this. She again glanced at her watch to see that the attack was ahead of schedule. She knew timing was always important but the explosion was what was expected; it was just early. She looked over the hedge again and it was as if someone had poked a hornet's nest. Sirens were sounding, floodlights had come on and soldiers were running everywhere. She decided to beat a hasty retreat back to the farm and make her escape.

5.50 pm

As Jeff Atkinson, the security man, climbed the steep steps up towards the escape door, the Stranger followed with Robert still in a headlock with the stiletto at his throat. He was about to tell the security man to go on up and unlock the door when there was a massive explosion. The security man literally flew back through the air, down the steps and knocked the two of them over. The Stranger lay there dazed and semi-conscious for several seconds. As he sat up and took stock of the situation he could see nothing because of the dust. He felt around and grabbed Robert and dragged him back to the bottom of the tunnel. Shouts further down the drive got louder and figures appeared out of the gloom.

'What the hell's going on?' said one of the workers.

'I don't know,' said the Stranger, 'we were checking the escape route and there was an explosion – I think that's what it was.'

At that moment the emergency siren sounded, and red flashing lights lit up the dust filled tunnel.

'Is that you, Robert?' the man said, looking at the prostrate body and kneeling down to inspect him. The Stranger kicked the man in the stomach and, as he folded and fell to the floor, he sank the stiletto into his back and twisted it.

The Stranger grabbed Robert, pulled him to his feet and slapped him hard several times. Robert started to come around and the Stranger dragged him back down the tunnel. When they were close to the instrument room the door crashed open and about twenty people ran out. They all looked scared out of their wits.

'Not to the escape shaft. The other way, out the entrance,' said the Stranger, and they ran off down the corridor.

The Stranger glanced through the door, saw the room was empty and dragged Robert in.

Sticking the knife into his ribs, he said to Robert, 'Now, listen to me very carefully. If you want your family to live, transmit this message to Station HX in Canada for onward transmission to Station IC in Iceland.'

Robert felt a sharp pain in his ribs that brought him around.

'Remember your family,' said the Stranger. 'If you want to see them again, prepare to transmit this now.'

In the dusty haze Robert could see his family drifting in front of him, beckoning him forward, beckoning him to join them. The point of the stiletto again brought him back from the brink.

'Now do it,' yelled the Stranger, his face red with anger, and he slapped Robert hard with his left hand.

'Now connect the output, HX Station, for onward transmission to IC. Now type this exactly,' he said. 'operation harpoon downgraded stop tirpitz in baltic on trials stop washington and wichita rendezvous 8 jan hvalfjorour stop caution u-boat activity expected stop.'

Robert typed the message onto punched tape, set the code destination and fed the punch tape into the transmitter.

He stared loathingly at the Stranger. 'Sent,' he said, and started smiling, then put his hand up as if to wave.

'Hello, Mother, hello Megan, look, they're coming ... can you see them? Thank you for sparing them,' he said, and he drifted into unconsciousness and tumbled off the chair onto the floor.

The Stranger stared at Robert, his own head already spinning, and before his very eyes the prostrate figure of Robert started to change into his father who stood up and raised his hand to hit him. The Stranger jumped back in horror and when he hit the floor he too was unconscious.

6.00 pm

At the top of the escape shaft, Dettsmann was trying to open the steel door that had only opened a crack. Being constructed of thick bars, the explosion had largely blown through the gaps and down the shaft.

'Shit,' he said, 'it won't budge!'

'Here,' said Hanke, bringing over a scaffolding pipe, 'let's use this.'

They both put their full weight on the pipe, using it as a lever, and the remainder of the lock cracked and broke free.

'In we go, lights on, and shoot anything that moves,' ordered Dettsmann.

They moved quickly but cautiously down the steps; the air was still full of dust and in the distance they could hear a siren waling. At the bottom of the first flight of stairs the tunnel turned at right angles and they were immediately presented with another locked steel bar door.

'Shit, shit, shit!' said Dettsmann as he shook it in vain, 'why the hell weren't we told about this one?'

Dettsmann shone his torch between the thick steel bars and could see nothing but dust.

'Right, let's get out of here fast. We don't have any explosives left to blow this one,' said Dettsmann, trying to organise his thoughts.

They climbed back up the steps quickly and looked to make sure it was still clear. Dettsmann realised they only had seconds before troops came to investigate the explosion and lack of radio reply. They jumped the sandbag wall and sprinted to the thick scrub to the east of the emplacement.

6.05 pm

Eleanor Bannencourt let herself back into the kitchen of Boswednack Farm. She recovered the transmitter and tuned into that night's frequency. When she established her contact she tapped in her final message: 'break in communication stop break in communication stop'. She waited for the acknowledgement and picked up the radio, took it to the yard and dropped it down the well. With the delayed splash she congratulated herself on a job well done. She picked up her rucksack, left the back door on the latch for the Stranger and headed west towards Nanjizal Bay.

6.05 pm
All hell had broken loose outside the Telegraph Station. Troops had been mustered and there was a sense of chaos as the majority of the troops were unaware of what was happening or what they had to do. The underground station had been shut down. Major Williams, the officer commanding Security Area 28, was trying to debrief the Company Commanders and the Security Team in the Telegraph House.

'Alright, quiet down, what's the latest, Staff Sergeant?' Williams demanded.

'Sir, gun fire was reported up at Boscarn Hamlets at around 5.40 pm. There was a single gunshot followed minutes later by small arms fire. That was followed a few minutes later by an explosion up above the Telegraph Station. Initial intelligence suggests that the door of the escape tunnel was blown open. The two soldiers guarding the escape tunnel are dead – both had their throats slit – and at one of the properties at Boscarn there's a dead German trooper and injured civilians including Harry Nancarrow, the local poacher. According to Harry, he killed another German trooper up at Polgassick Farm, but we're checking on that.'

The Major swept his fingers through his hair; he couldn't take it all in. 'Two of my soldiers with their throats cut, an explosion, gun fire, injured civilians and two dead Germans. What the bloody hell is happening here?' he demanded.

He was in overload.

'Major,' said Bert, 'that was me.'

'What was? Who are you, Granddad?' barked the Major dismissively.

Bert looked fixedly at the Major, not best pleased. 'Bert Chenoweth, sir, Sergeant, Home Guard. I shot the German in my kitchen. He was holding my family hostage. I shot him through the kitchen window.'

'Whoah, whoah, not so fast, sergeant, take me through what happened.'

'Sir, I was patrolling the upper path to the west of the village and I heard someone yelling my name – it was Harry Nancarrow from up St Levan, he's the local poacher.

He was running down Main Road like he was being chased by demons and I couldn't catch him or make him hear – I'm not as fast as I used to be. I saw him get to my house and when the door opened and he was dragged inside I knew there was a problem. I went around the back and looked through the kitchen window and the German soldier had everyone tied up and a knife at my Clara's throat, so I shot him. It's a bit of a mess, sir. I shot him in the head with my 303.'

'Christ, sergeant, what the hell are you trying to tell me? Who was in the kitchen?' barked the Major.

'The German soldier, sir, with Clara my daughter-in-law, Megan, May and Harry. That's not the half of it. The thing is, sir, there are other Germans and an enemy agent.'

'There's what?' exclaimed the Major, deciding to sit down and still having trouble taking in the avalanche of information.

'Yes, sir. Robert, my Grandson, works at the Telegraph, and the enemy agent kidnapped him, I think, to gain access to the underground Telegraph, and there was a German officer as well as the one I shot.'

'Hang on, sergeant, you're telling me there were two Germans and an enemy agent at your house?'

'Well, sir, actually three, I believe, but of course I wasn't there at the time. I think this explains why my cockerel went missing a few days back.'

'Christ Almighty,' said Williams, almost apoplectic and shaking his head.

'So the enemy agent took your grandson hostage, you shot one German, so where's the German officer and the other German soldier, and what's a fucking cockerel got to do with it?'

'Sir,' interrupted the Staff Sergeant, trying to calm the situation. 'I think the German officer, and probably others, are responsible for killing the two guards and blowing the escape door, and the likelihood is that they have accessed the under-ground Telegraph Station.'

'So why did the enemy agent take the boy hostage?' the Major asked, exasperated.

'It must have been to gain access to the Telegraph,' said the Staff Sergeant.

'But you're telling me they blew the bloody escape door to gain access?' said the Major, now speaking several octaves higher. 'Jesus Christ, bring me the access register,' he instructed, suddenly aware of the magnitude of what was unfolding.

He ran his finger down the list and read, '5.31 pm R Chenoweth and J Tregembo.'

'Chenoweth is my grandson, and Tregembo has been missing for over a week,' said Bert.

'Oh shit,' said the Major, 'that means there has been a breach of security.'

'Put me through to the War Cabinet immediately, priority one, not a moment to waste.'

'If that bastard has hurt my Robert I'll personally—' but Bert didn't finish the statement, no one was listening.

6.35 pm
Fifteen minutes, later Major Williams returned.

'All hell has broken out in London over this – even Churchill is involved. I hope no one was planning any sleep tonight. OK listen up: a colonel from Intelligence happens to be at RAF Sennen. Staff Sergeant, send a car with your best driver and a couple of armed soldiers over to Sennen and pick up Colonel Bonham somebody-or-other and bring him here immediately. And take an armed escort vehicle. If there are Germans around we don't want top-brass being bumped off as well.'

'Right, we need to get access to the underground Telegraph before these bastards destroy the equipment if they haven't already done so,' said the Major.

'Sir, when the alarm system was triggered, the instrument room was flooded with Agent 15. I don't think anyone in there is a threat – they'll all be fast asleep, dreaming of the Fatherland,' said the Staff Sergeant with relish.

'In your dreams, sergeant. The Germans don't send a bunch of amateurs on a mission like this. They'll be trained and hardened combatants. They'll have gas masks. I want a red alert immediately for all of Security Area 28, and phone the surrounding Areas and tell them to go to amber alert. How quickly can we get back in, sergeant?'

6.35 pm

Dettsmann and Hanke were laying low one field east of the escape shaft. What to do? he wondered. With the confusion in the valley there was still an opportunity to create a diversion and cause some serious damage. He'd thought of going back down the escape shaft and using their hand grenades to blow the door but he guessed that it would now be overrun with soldiers. The only answer was a commando-style raid on the main entrance to the underground Telegraph. They had to make sure the message had been sent and most importantly destroy what they could of the facility.

He pulled out a length of rope, tied one end to a fence post and threw it over the cliff. He nodded to Hanke to follow him and slid over the edge directly behind Telegraph House.

6.35 pm

Almost directly below the two Germans, Major Williams was still in Telegraph House with his team. He was trying to assimilate the information but much of it was either sketchy, unsubstantiated or contradictory. He was having a job tying any of it together.

The phone on his desk rang. 'Yes?' he barked.

'Sir, the gas is clear and it's safe to re-enter,' said the voice at the other end.

'Good,' he said, preferring action over briefings. 'Right, let's go, on the double, there's not a second to lose, I want the security squad at the tunnel door in one minute.'

He picked up his machine gun and stormed out of the office.

'I'm coming with you,' said Bert. 'I have to know if Robert is alright.'

6.45 pm

As Major Williams and the others reached the tunnel, the two bombproof doors were wide open to allow as much ventilation through the facility as possible to clear the last of the gas. The air draught was so strong they could feel it pushing against their backs as they entered. Guns raised, they cautiously progressed down the tunnel. Two minutes later they peered into the instrument room and clearly visible were two figures lying on the floor.

'Staff Sergeant, you and two others work forward towards the emergency exit, and be careful – check for booby traps,' ordered the Major.

He reached forward and threw open the instrument room door. All was quiet, so he peered in and, with machine gun raised, entered the room. He was relieved to see that the facility appeared undamaged and carefully worked his way around the room.

At the transmission desk he checked the two unconscious civilians.

'Quick, over here,' he said, and beckoned the Staff Sergeant and two soldiers. Bert followed behind them and made straight for Robert. He knelt beside him, rolled him over and to his horror saw his blood-stained face and shirt.

He put his ear to his chest. 'He's still breathing,' yelled Bert.

He and the sergeant pulled Robert into a sitting position and started slapping him on the face.

'Robert, are you OK? Wake up, Robert ... Robert wake up,' he said excitedly. Robert groaned and, looking dazed, responded with a mumble.

'Oh, thank God,' said Bert. 'It's OK, Robert, you're going to be fine.'

The sergeant turned his attention to the Stranger, who was starting to stir. He tied his hands behind his back and roughly sat him up and slapped him repeatedly.

'Wake up, you scumbag,' he grizzled.

'So this our man,' said the Major giving him a firm prod in the ribs with his machine gun barrel to test his status.

Bert stared at him, and the gash on the forehead confirmed the Stranger's identity. 'That's the bastard that kidnapped my family,' he said coldly.

'Sir, no sign of any Germans,' said the Staff Sergeant. 'We've searched the whole underground facility and we've found Atkinson the security man and Collins the telegrapher both dead at the bottom of the escape shaft but no one else. There are certainly no Germans in the facility – the intermediate door was still locked, they couldn't get in.'

'Right, I want this guy out to the Telegraph House for interrogation pronto,' said the Major.

A flash of realisation went through the Stranger's mind. So the other troopers are still at large, perhaps all was not lost, he thought.

6.45 pm

Dettsmann and Hanke were over the cliff and on the ground in a matter of seconds. They kept between the cliff and the back of the Telegraph House building, worked their way uphill and at the end of the building stopped and surveyed the area. They saw a group of soldiers running down the road and out of sight. Other soldiers were milling around in a disorganised fashion.

Dettsmann said, 'Hanke, there's a guard post over there. You work your way around to the right behind that low wall and let me know when you're in place. Then on my signal lob in a grenade – I'll pick off the stragglers. That should set the cat amongst the pigeons ... then we'll move up the east side of the road to the tunnel entrance.'

6.55 pm

Robert was now sitting up but looking groggy.

He gasped and looked at Bert. 'Megan and—' he said, trying to remember names, 'are they—?'

'Yes, Robert, they're all OK. A bit shaken but they're all well. Megan, May and Clara, they're all OK.'

Roberts's shoulders started to heave and he let out a huge sob. 'Oh thank God,' he said, 'thank God, I thought they were done for.'

Bert put an arm on his shoulder and felt tears in his own eyes through the sheer raw emotion.

'They're all OK, Robert. Now tell us what happened here.'

Wiping tears from his eyes, he had another flashback. 'The enemy agent,' said Robert, 'he's dangerous, he's got a knife, he's the one that killed Josh Tregembo, he's a cold-hearted animal.'

'We've got him. He's right here. He can do no more harm to anyone.'

Robert looked around and latched onto the Stranger who was being removed and he shouted angrily after him: 'Whoever you are, you're going to get your fuckin' neck stretched, you unspeakable piece of Nazi shit. You killed Josh and would have done for my family. They're just harmless village folk.'

The Stranger looked at him without a trace of emotion and was frogmarched unceremoniously down the tunnel to the entrance.

6.55 pm

Hanke crawled off, keeping as low a profile as possible. The whole area was now brightly illuminated by the security lights and it took him several minutes to crawl to the guard post. At that moment, Dettsmann saw a group of soldiers and a civilian exit the tunnel and walk towards Telegraph House.

Is it? It looks like ... it is ... it's Stiletto, he thought.

He signalled to Hanke and five seconds later there was an explosion and then the screams and moans of wounded men. Several soldiers who'd escaped the worst of the blast scattered, and Dettsmann clinically sprayed them with submachine gun fire and ran forwards, still shooting. Hanke flanked right and joined in. The Stranger ran towards them with his hands still tied behind him, but limping. Hanke was about to shoot him but recognised the coat and instead grabbed him and dragged him behind the sandbags of the guard post he'd just destroyed.

'Get this bloody rope off,' said the Stranger, and Hanke cut him free.

His left leg hurt like hell and he lifted his trouser leg to see he'd got a bullet wound in the calf. He pulled out his handkerchief to tie around the wound.

Dettsmann joined them and said, 'Has the message been sent and is the facility destroyed?'

'Yes, the message is sent but they gassed us before I could destroy the equipment,' replied the Stranger.

'Shit,' muttered Dettsmann, 'we'll have to go in and finish the job.'

He signalled Hanke to move forward in the direction of the tunnel entrance. They moved off down the road, returning fire that came from the security checkpoint. The Stranger had been distracted by tying his handkerchief tightly around his wound, and when he looked up they were twenty paces away and he immediately saw the danger.

No not that way,' he yelled, but it was too late; neither grasped the shouted English.

They ran towards the building with the Bus Stop sign on the roof for some cover. As they approached, what had appeared to be a window dropped open and a machine gun crackled. It was the last thing the two ever saw. Firing at five hundred rounds a minute, the five-second burst ripped them to pieces.

The Stranger watched the slaughter of his comrades with alarm and shock and realised he was now on his own and very vulnerable. Keeping low, he slipped back into the shadows between the cliff and the Telegraph House, limping painfully.

There was a rope hanging down the cliff and he realised that was how his colleagues had got down. He wasted no time, grabbed the rope and climbed hand-over-hand with his feet slipping on the muddy rock surface, dislodging rocks that rattled down the cliff. As he scrambled the last couple of feet over the cliff edge, bullets zinged off the rocks around him and over his head.

Monday 5 January 1942 – 7.00 pm
Critical Communication, Porthcurno

Colonel Julian Bonham-Johns arrived at the Telegraph House in the middle of the fire fight.

'We need to hole up here until this is sorted,' said Hunt.

'There's no time to lose,' said Bonham-Johns pulling his pistol from the holster and started to trot down the road.

'Shit,' muttered Hunt, 'for Christ's sake, sir, they're shooting at anything that moves.'

With that, the cliff above the Telegraph House erupted in ricocheting bullets and they all dived for cover. Hunt saw a group of soldiers sheltering behind a wall and taking potshots at the cliff top.

'Hey you, yes you, come with us.' He said it with such menace and authority they didn't question his instruction.

'Quick,' he said, 'follow the colonel,' who was already thirty yards ahead of them. He figured if they were part of a group of soldiers they were less likely to be shot at.

7.00 pm
Up above them, the Stranger lay low for several seconds, catching his breath, and pulled up the rope; he didn't want to be followed. Bullets whistled over his head. Then a searchlight scanned the crest of the cliff and the accompanying gunfire and bullets was deafening. He was pleased he'd lifted the rope as that would have given his position away. Fortunately for him, the shooting was not accurate. Slithering away from the crest he got into thick gorse and scrub and stopped to attend to his leg. It was just a flesh wound in the calf but would slow him down. He re-tied the handkerchief more tightly and moved off, working his way north along the line of the cliff edge.

7.05 pm
Bonham-Johns reached the security doors a few seconds before the group of soldiers.

'Halt,' yelled a nervous young soldier waving his rifle.

'Easy, soldier,' said Bonham-Johns, 'we're from National Intelligence. Major Williams is expecting us.'

The soldier didn't even know who Major Williams was and continued to point his rifle at the colonel, very uncertain of what to do.

'Soldier,' yelled Hunt, 'put that bloody rifle down before I have you court-martialled and shot.' He immediately lowered his gun and stepped back.

How the hell does he do that? thought Bonham-Johns. That is impressive.

'Stay here and await further instructions,' yelled Hunt at the group of soldiers, and he and the colonel pushed past the doors and raced down the tunnel.

7.10 pm

In the instrument room, Robert was sitting in a chair holding his head, with Bert supporting him. Bonham-Johns introduced himself to Major Williams and asked for a rundown on the security compromise.

'This is the man who can give you the background verbatim,' said the Major. 'This is Robert Chenoweth. He was kidnapped by what appears to be an enemy agent who forced him at knifepoint to come in here.'

'Robert, tell me what happened. I need all the details – leave nothing out,' said Bonham-Johns in a kindly tone. He could see Robert was in shock, and his neck and shirt was covered in blood.

'Well, sir, we were at home and this man and some Germans came in. They held my family hostage and forced me to come down here.'

'I understand your family is fine, but tell me how you gained access to the Telegraph?' asked Bonham-Johns.

'I'm the Shift Manager here and I have a pass. He had Josh Tregembo's pass that he'd altered, and that got him in.'

'Who's Josh Tregembo?' asked Bonham-Johns.

'He was the Cipher Supervisor here and he went missing on Christmas Eve, that bastard kidnapped him and took his pass.'

167

'You came in together?'

'Yes, I'm sorry, sir ... he had a knife in my ribs.' Gingerly, Robert raised his arm to show his slashed and blood-stained shirt.

'Robert, you couldn't have done anything else, no one could,' said Bonham-Johns. 'Now please, go on.'

'We went to Jeff's office.'

'Sorry, who is Jeff?'

'Jeff Atkinson, the head of security. He got Jeff to take the escape door key out of the safe and as we were walking up the steps to unlock the door there was a big, well explosion I think, I can't really remember.'

'So you were going to unlock the emergency escape door, and someone blew the door at that moment?'

Robert nodded vaguely; he couldn't quite piece it together. Bonham-Johns couldn't grasp it either; why had they wanted to unlock a door from inside when it was being blown open from the outside? It didn't make sense.

'And then?' he asked, moving on.

'When we'd recovered from the blast, he forced me back to the instrument room to send a message to IC Iceland via HX Canada, that's Nova Scotia.'

'Oh bloody hell,' said Bonham-Johns, putting his head in his hands, 'why didn't I see that coming? Are you sure it was to Iceland?'

'Yes,' said Robert, 'HX is the Canadian terminus of the transatlantic cable, and they have an onward deep sea cable to Iceland.'

'What was the message, Robert?'

Robert rubbed his eyes and tried to recall the message. 'I'm not exactly sure.'

'This is critical,' urged Bonham-Johns. 'You have to try and remember.'

'Sorry, I just don't know, but there will be a punch tape copy of it on the transmitter.'

'Show me,' said Bonham-Johns, and with his arm around Robert, the two of them went across to a pile of punched tape in a large tray.

'Here it is,' Robert said, 'the last message. It reads, "operation harpoon downgraded stop tirpitz in baltic on trials stop washington and wichita rendezvous 8 jan hvalfjorour stop caution u-boat activity expected stop".'

Bonham-Johns thought hard about what he'd just heard and was muttering to himself.

'So the Germans want us to divert the two American battleships away from Scapa Flow to Iceland – why? Could the inference be to support the Arctic Convoys? But they've not mentioned PQ7B . . . Are the Nazis so brazen as to try and take on the battleships and PQ7B at the same time? That doesn't seem likely.'

His heart was pounding.

'Surely it can only be to move the two battleships away from the northern North Sea to allow Tirpitz to escape to Trondheim? It's got to be.'

Turning to Hunt he said, 'Now, this is critical. What's the date today?'

'Monday 5th January, sir,' said Hunt, checking his watch.

'OK, they want Washington and Wichita to be in Hvalfjörður on the 8th. It's a two-day sail so the two battleships will have to leave tomorrow, that's the 6th. Let's say Tirpitz will wait in dock until they are one day into the sailing and will then depart Wilhelmshaven for Trondheim.'

'But, colonel, the message says that Tirpitz is in the Baltic,' said Hunt.

'Yes, I know, I know, but it has to be a bluff. Everything points towards it making for Norway – that's where the action is. Germany desperately wants to break the Arctic Convoys that are feeding the eastern front.'

Christ, I don't know what to make of all this, Bonham-Johns thought. He looked up and saw Robert's blood-stained face, the Major, the Staff Sergeant and Hunt all staring at him. They needed guidance, and he realised he had to make a decision.

'Right,' said Bonham-Johns, 'if we have her speed assessed accurately it'll take her close to two days to get to Trondheim and will pass Scapa Flow, with Washington and Wichita already a day away. So she'd sail on the 7th January and be in Trondheim on the 9th.'

'The cunning buggers,' said Hunt.

'Christ, that's the day after tomorrow and that coincides with the next bad weather coming in, the best time for her to sail. Damn it, if we only had another day or so to allow Tuscaloosa to reach Sullom Voe and replenish. Christ, this is going to be tight, Robert,' said Bonham-Johns.

Robert didn't have a clue what he was talking about.

'Oh yes, sir, I just remembered. I did send the message via HX Nova Scotia but not to IC Iceland but to CI Jersey. That line has been dead since the German invasion last year. I thought if he wanted to send that message it must be very important to the Nazis so I sent it, but to the wrong destination.'

Bonham-Johns looked at him, incredulous.

'You mean you didn't send the message to Iceland? Robert, are you sure, absolutely sure?'

'Yes, sir, one hundred percent,' said Robert rather nervously, not sure now if he'd done the right thing.

'Is there anyone to receive the message in Jersey?' asked Bonham-Johns.

'No, I don't think so, I think the facility was destroyed at the beginning of the occupation,' replied Robert.

'Oh Robert, that was brave of you and exactly the right thing to do, you have done well,' he added. 'OK, that means we have to resend the message, this time via Nova Scotia to Iceland without delay. We need to make sure the Nazi mole in Iceland gets wind of this.'

Robert looked at him quizzically, not understanding.

'Robert this is a key communication. I know it sounds odd, but this transmission will be intercepted by the Germans. You can bet there is some recognition code tied up in it.'

'But why send it if the Germans will intercept it? That doesn't make sense,' queried Robert.

'It's all about timing, Robert. Tirpitz is ready to sail – that's why the Germans want to get this message out. The Germans are sending this message to persuade us to recall two US battleships intended to hunt down Tirpitz in the North Sea. With them out of the way, it will allow Tirpitz to escape Wilhelmshaven and make for Trondheim in relative safety. But they don't know about our trump card, USS Tuscaloosa, and we want to be in control of the timing so we can attack Tirpitz and destroy her. The problem is we're not quite ready, and we need to delay her departure a day so that Tuscaloosa is replenished and ready to confront her.

'Resend the message, Robert, to HX Station for onward transmission to IC but this time say, "operation harpoon downgraded stop tirpitz in baltic on trials stop washington and wichita rendezvous 9 jan hvalfjorour stop caution u-boat activity expected stop". Do you see any possible encryption in the message that would stop us sending it?'

'No, sir, not if we're changing only the date,' said Robert.

'Mm, yes I see that, so Robert, we'll just have to risk it. Send it now to HX for forward transmission to IC. Trust me, Robert, this is a breakthrough that might change the course of the war and it's thanks to your heroism.' Robert smiled for the first time that afternoon.

Bonham-Johns continued outlining the plan. 'When you have sent that message, we must shut down everything for at least three days until Tirpitz sails, and I'll clear that with Churchill. The Nazis have to think they've destroyed the facility. Robert, I then need you to send a secure coded message to Naval Command, Devonport.'

7.45 pm

The Stranger could hear soldiers not far away and hid in a gorse thicket, pistol at the ready. The soldiers passed by on the track twenty feet away. His heart was in his mouth. When they had gone, he moved forward and could see the sandbag emplacement around the escape shaft about one hundred yards further on. He gave it a wide berth and hugged the hedge to work his way up to Boscarn Hamlets. He had some unfinished business, he was feeling vengeful, but realised he couldn't stay there for long.

7.45 pm

The Staff Sergeant ran back into the instrument room.

'Sir, the prisoner has escaped,' he said, breathless.

'What?' said Major Williams, shaking his head in disbelief.

'Sir, there was a gun battle. The German troops attempted to free him, they are both dead but he's disappeared.'

'How the hell can he just bloody disappear?' barked the Major.

'Christ this is serious,' said Bonham-Johns, 'we've got to find him. If he gets to a radio, our cover will be blown.'

'Colonel,' interrupted Bert, 'can I have a word? I think I know where he might be going.'

'Who are you?' he asked.

'I'm Bert Chenoweth, Robert's grandfather and a sergeant in the Home Guard Area Security Team. I've come across this guy before.'

'So you think you can find him, Bert?'

'Well I can't guarantee it, sir, but I'm pretty sure.'

'OK, how many soldiers do we need?'

'Sir, just me and Will. If he's where I think he is, we know the location far better than anyone else, and we'll track him down – and more importantly, we won't spook him.'

'Right, count me in, Bert, but you call the shots. Hunt, you stay here and send a secure coded message to Churchill at Naval Command, Devonport. Tell him everything. I'll speak with him personally as soon as I get back. Sergeant, we need extra ammo, and give me that Browning and a couple of extra clips,' said Bonham-Johns. 'Lead the way, Bert.'

Monday 5 January 1942 – 6.00 pm
Noordwijk, occupied Netherlands

Wenger was distracted from the task in hand. He had not been himself since his experience in Pontchâteau. He was troubled that the Nazi High Command seemed suspicious and distrustful of their Abwehr work. He wondered how many of the messages he'd sent to Berlin were actually read, let alone acted upon.

'To hell with them,' he muttered, and his thoughts turned to the lovely Caja, and his sense of well-being was heightened by the fact that in her note to him she had forgiven him for not meeting her last Wednesday. She seemed impressed that he'd met with such important people. She said that her friend's room was still available and they could spend the night there. They arranged to meet at 9 pm in De Oude Molen. He was imagining being squeezed into the small bed next to her naked body.

Stefan Merensky passed Wenger a message and said, 'Captain, this is the first of the messages we're expecting. It was picked up at 6.05 pm.'

It was from Agent Banjo, and the code 'Break in Communication' confirmed that the attack on Porthcurno Telegraph Station was underway. This was Wenger's cue to monitor and confirm a message from Porthcurno to Iceland via Halifax, Nova Scotia. The message was to be immediately transcribed and sent to Berlin.

Whilst he waited for the crucial second message, he read through some of the other communications without really focusing. Caja was foremost in his mind tonight; she was the only thing that mattered. He'd missed two opportunities to sleep with her and was not going to miss a third.

Two hours later, the expected second message had still not arrived, and he kept glancing at his watch. Come on, he thought, where the hell is it? Again he glanced at his watch, 8.03, and again at 8.05, but still nothing.

At 8.15 pm Merensky said, 'The message has just come in, sir.'

'About bloody time. Pass it here quickly.'

Wenger studied the message. It came from their contact in Iceland and reported the transmission from PK to IC via HX was received at 7.40 pm. He was puzzled by the time difference between the two messages. The first had been picked up at 6.05 from Agent Banjo and confirmed the attack on Porthcurno Telegraph Station had started. The second message had been sent an hour and thirty-five minutes later. Why such a delay?

Wenger glanced at his watch again, and his heart missed a beat. Who knows why it was late? he thought, and at that moment he really didn't care. He only had one thing on his mind.

He then communicated to Berlin by Enigma code to confirm that Iceland had received the expected message from Agent Stiletto and sent a copy of the transmission.

He looked at his watch and said to the team, 'I'm off, see you bright and early in the morning.'

Monday 5 January 1942 – 8.00 pm

The Chase, Porthcurno

8.00 pm

When the Stranger got close to the back of Boscarn Hamlets, his heart sank. There were soldiers in the back garden guarding the area. He'd concluded that the occupants might not have been killed, given the snippets of information he'd overheard. He weighed up his options. He could kill as many soldiers as possible and get into number three and dispatch any of the remaining family. But they were probably receiving medical attention somewhere else, and he had an important rendezvous in just two hours.

Reluctantly, he decided to bypass the area and head for Fern Cottage as quickly as he could.

8.00 pm

Bert and Bonham-Johns left the Telegraph and walked as fast as Bert could manage up the hill to the village hall.

'Ah, Will, there you are. Come with us, mate, we've got a job to finish. Oh, and this is the colonel. He's coming with us. Colonel, this is Will Tarraway.'

'What's up?' asked Will. 'There's a lot of commotion going on, and we were asked to remain here on standby.'

'Job to be done, like we did on those raids before Delville Wood in 1916. We need to take a prisoner.'

Bonham-Johns instantly realised that the two old men had been war heroes in a previous era and had put their lives on the line when he was a babe in arms. He was full of admiration.

They turned left off the main street and up the steep hill towards St Levan. The light was fair with the moon at full quarter, but passing clouds plunged the area into intermittent darkness; a good night for tracking, thought Bert. In ten minutes they reached the field above St Levan church and they dropped behind the hedge to catch their breath. All Bert could hear was the thump, thump, thump of his heartbeat. He didn't stand a chance of hearing anything else. Deep breaths, he said to himself. Deep breaths, old man. Will was no better.

A few minutes later, they were ready to move on. Bert moved to a gate and carefully glanced into the village. He could see nothing and waited for the cloud to pass. When the moon shone through, he surveyed the area.

'Nothing. Let's move towards the church,' he whispered. They hid behind the graveyard wall and waited in silence.

'OK,' whispered Bert, 'it doesn't look like he's here but you two go on to the farm, I just want to check something in the village quickly.'

'No, we stick together,' whispered Bonham-Johns.

'Sir, you go on with Will. I just have to check something.'

'No, Bert, we stick together.'

'Who's calling the shots here?' asked Bert, rather irritated.

'You are, Bert, but we stay together, is that clear?'

Bert glared at Bonham-Johns. 'OK, you stay out of sight here. Will, you watch out for me coming back.'

8.20 pm

The Stranger waited several minutes on the east side of the Porthcurno Road to make sure it was safe to cross. After he'd done so, he made steady progress west across the fields. He tried to balance keeping out of sight by following the hedges with making up for lost time by heading across fields. Ten minutes later and limping badly with the pain in his calf muscle, he dropped down into the copse just on the north of St Levan church and stopped and listened. He felt uneasy. He had taken rather too many risks because he was behind schedule. Attention to detail, he thought to himself, always attention to detail.

He held his breath and listened. Very faintly, almost imperceptibly, he thought he heard muted voices in conversation. It was too dangerous to hang around, so he hobbled to Fern Cottage and slipped around the building through the back garden and onto the track he used to get to and from Boswednack Farm.

8.40 pm

Bert crossed the graveyard, keeping low behind the gravestones. To one side of the graveyard lay the St Levan Stone, a large, round, granite boulder that was split in two. Bert had hidden there many times as a child to avoid Sunday school but now it offered him a hiding place with more sinister intent. He slid into the gap with his rifle pointing forward and watched the path.

Moments later, he caught some movement on the path below. He closed his eyes to accustom them to the dark and looked again. Yes, there you are you bastard, he thought, he's come from the direction of Fern Cottage. He waited a couple of minutes for the Stranger to move on and then worked towards the house.

All was in complete darkness. He cautiously tried the back door but it was locked. He stood back and gave it a strong kick. There was the sound of splitting wood but the door remained tight. His leg hurt from the impact.

'Bugger this getting old bullshit,' he muttered. He kicked again, using his other leg, which hurt even more, but this time the door swung open. He pulled out the torch and entered the kitchen. He searched the two downstairs rooms but found nothing. He mounted the narrow staircase and checked the two bedrooms: again, nothing. As he exited, there was a noise and sudden movement by his feet that made him start. He fell backwards and saw a large rat in the torch beam. Shit, he thought. As he painfully got up, two more rats ran from the old shed across the yard.

As he approached, there was a stench that he recognised from those terrible years in the trenches; it was unmistakeably human. He knocked the padlock off the shed door and shone his torch in and saw nothing immediately ... but then in the far corner, his light fell on a tarpaulin. His heart was thumping with the expectation. He grabbed the corner and pulled it hard and ran out into the fresh air. The stench was overwhelming but when he shone his light on it there was nothing. Holding his nose he again checked the shed a second time, but nothing.

'Shit,' he muttered. He looked behind the shed but found nothing and decided to return to his colleagues. As he crossed the back garden, he saw the circular stone well. As he approached, the stench increased. He knocked wooden planks off the top, turned away, took a deep breath of fresh air and looked over the edge, shining his torch into the inky blackness. Ten feet down, he could see the surface of the water and something splashing around, and as he was trying to focus, two fat wet rats leapt from the well and over his shoulder. He was no stranger to rats but he reeled back at the horror of it and gagged. Taking a couple of deep breaths, he shone his torch into the well and there it was: a bloated body with a shock of ginger hair clearly visible.

He had found Josh Tregembo.

His heart sank and the life went out of his legs and he collapsed on the ground.

'Oh my God,' he muttered. 'The poor little bugger. What the hell happened? Why poor Josh? Such a lovely lad. He was just doing his job. If I get my hands on that fucking scumbag I'll make sure he pays.'

An anger gripped him that he hadn't experienced for many years and it brought strength back to his legs. With renewed purpose, Bert picked up his rifle and moved off quickly to find Will and Bonham-Johns.

8.55 pm
Slipping in behind the St Levan Stone, Bert made a high-pitched squealing noise and waited. A few seconds later, Will responded with the same and Bert broke cover and joined them.

'OK, the Stranger moved out about five, maybe six, minutes ago heading up the gully towards Boswednack Farm. The good news is there's no evidence of a radio and I don't think he's carrying one, so it'll be at the farmhouse. The bad news is I've found Josh Tregembo – he's dead. We'll head across Long Meadow. Not so much cover but faster than following him through the gully. I want to get ahead of him and cut him off.'

Bert didn't even wait for a reply and headed off at a fast pace that made even Bonham-Johns short of breath. Will's lungs were burning and he had an uneasy feeling. He'd seen Bert singly focused on vengeance before and he knew that on such rare occasions he was unstoppable and that blood would be spilled. He just hoped it wouldn't be theirs.

They waited for what seemed an age but as Bert had predicted they eventually caught a glimpse of a shadow moving across the adjacent field to their right. They ran along the hedge out of sight but parallel with the shadowy figure and then cut right along the hedge at the end of the field. They waited and waited and Bert thought everyone within a hundred yards would hear his thumping heart and deep breathing. He was stifling a cough. They waited in silence and Bert wondered if he'd doubled back.

A fox barked in the distance and faintly, very faintly, they could hear the waves breaking on the rocks of Nanjizal Bay. And then clouds scudded over and blocked the moonlight. Shit, that's when he'll make his move, thought Bert, and in anticipation he crawled forward, lay on the wet grass and aimed his rifle ahead. The scudding clouds cleared and sure enough, there, a hundred feet in front, a figure was bathed in moonlight.

'Halt,' yelled Bert, 'or I'll blow your fucking brains out.'

Bonham-Johns was taken aback by the cold ferocity of Bert's warning. The figure froze.

'Stand with your hands in the air, feet apart,' ordered Bert, but the figure did not move. Bert squeezed the trigger of his rifle and the bullet buzzed a couple of feet from the figure's head.

'Put your hands up, I said,' and slowly the figure stood upright.

'I said put your hands up, last warning.'

'I can't,' said the figure. 'I've a broken right arm.'

'Put your left arm up then,' Bert said, but the figure didn't move.

'Will, you keep the bastard covered from the right.' Bert got up and moved towards the figure.

'Who are you?' he demanded, but there was no reply. Bert walked left towards the figure and flashed his torch in his face.

Clearly seeing the gash on his forehead, he spat out, 'You, you bastard,' he said. 'Rodney Lavine, or what other names do you go by? You know I should shoot you right now.'

'We need him alive, Bert,' said Bonham-Johns.

'There you are, you see, you can't shoot an unarmed civilian,' said the Stranger, 'it's against the Geneva Convention.'

'Fuck the convention,' said Bert, 'it's not there to protect scum like you.'

'Hey man, you've got this wrong. I'm just going to visit Mrs Bannencourt before I head home tomorrow.'

'And where might that be? Berlin or some other fucking Nazi rathole?' spat Bert.

'I said I'm just going over to Boswednack Farm to see Mrs Bannencourt,' repeated the Stranger.

'You're not English are you? I can hear a South African accent.'

'Yes, you got me,' he said. 'I spent ten years on the gold mines at Langlaagte. I'm a mining engineer.'

'You lying bastard. I fought with fine boys from the South African Infantry Brigade at Delville Wood and they talked about traitorous scum like you. You kidnapped and tortured my family and killed Jeff Atkinson, and for that you should be hanged. But you also killed Josh Tregembo, you evil bastard, and for that I'm going to kill you myself, no need for a trial.'

'Sergeant,' barked Bonham-Johns, 'that's enough.'

'Turn around and start walking to the farm. We want to talk with your lady-friend as well. Come on, get moving, back across the field,' Bert snarled.

Instead of moving forward, the Stranger just stood there.

'I can't move my right arm,' said the Stranger, and in that instant, he swung around and a shot rang out. The bullet buzzed past Bert's ear followed by two more shots and then a click, click, click. The pistol was empty. The last two bullets had been aimed at the other two, and Will cried out.

'Will, are you alright?' yelled Bonham-Johns.

'No I've been fuckin' hit.'

'Where?'

'I don't know, the arm I think. Shit, that bloody hurts.'

In the commotion the Stranger had started to run, but the moon was not on his side and shone down brightly on his hapless figure. Bert raised his Lee-Enfield rifle, said nothing, took aim and pulled the trigger. The bullet hit the Stranger square in the back, and his dead body thumped into the ground. It was twenty-three years since Bert had been in combat and he had vowed never to do so again. Now he'd killed twice in one day. He felt the bile rise in his stomach and retched.

'That was supposed to be the war that ended all wars. Now look at this bloody mess, you stupid bastards,' he yelled. 'How the hell did this fucking bullshit start all over again?' He shook his head as if to clear some demons from his mind.

'You got what you deserved, you bastard,' he reminded himself, 'but I have to live with the memory.'

Bonham-Johns was tending to Will when Bert came over.

'You alright, Will?' queried Bert.

'Bloody sore, since you ask. The same fucking arm I got shot in last time.'

'He'll be fine,' said Bonham-Johns, 'I think it's a flesh wound but he will need medical attention.'

'Will, you head back to Porthcurno, report this shooting and get that arm seen to. The colonel and I will go onto the farm.'

'Not a chance, I'm coming with you,' said Will.

Bert said firmly, 'Listen, Will, bullet wounds and old men don't go together. Your priority is to get back to your Bessie. Trust me, you don't take chances on that.'

Will looked at him and knew he was right.

'OK, just this once,' said Will.

Bonham-Johns was checking the Stranger for any papers or belongings that might shed light on the situation, but there was nothing except a mean-looking steel stiletto knife, the Webley snub-nosed pistol and a piece of card with a hand-written telephone number: Mayfair 3349. He looked at the number in disbelief. He felt numb at the thought, and a wave of complicit guilt flushed his cheeks.

9.20 pm
Bonham-Johns was in shock and just stood there.

'OK, let's go, colonel,' said Bert.

But he didn't move.

'Now, colonel,' repeated Bert.

Bonham-Johns pulled himself together.

'After you, Bert, you lead the way,' he said.

Within five minutes they'd arrived at the farmhouse. Bert moved to the back door, clicked the latch gently and pushed, and to his surprise it swung open with a low-pitched creak. He shone his torch around the kitchen. There was a dirty plate and mug on the table; the Cornish Range was still hot.

'Wait here,' said Bert. 'I'll see if our Mrs Bannencourt has left anything of interest.'

When Bert had finished searching, he said, 'Well, she's gone, but I know where the Germans were holed-up before the raid – look over here.'

Bert pointed down the steps to a cellar, and Bonham-Johns climbed down.

'You could hide an army down here,' he said.

Bert looked at his watch and thought about their next move.

'Christ, you know what, it's less than an hour to high tide … could they possibly be escaping by sea?' he asked.

Bonham-Johns looked quizzical and said, 'Where's the best location for a U-boat pick-up?'

'Most of the coast is either mined or has high cliffs,' said Bert. 'The only possible location is Nanjizal Bay.'

'What are we waiting for? There's not a moment to lose. Lead the way, Bert.'

9.35 pm

Bert started at a fast pace, but was soon gasping, his lungs burning. He stopped with a hacking cough and fell to his knees.

'Old age and a whiff of gas in '16,' he spluttered apologetically.

'Come on, Bert, you're a bloody hero,' said Bonham-Johns, lifting him under his arm. 'The security of the nation depends on us. You don't know how much your country is relying on you right now. If I'm right she's got information of national importance.'

9.55 pm

At the cliff edge they peered out to sea. The moon made the surface shimmer and twinkle, but they could see nothing.

'Let's try further along,' said Bert.

They stared again but nothing.

Bonham-Johns was surveying the sea further to their right.

'Look there, Bert.'

As they watched, a U-boat was surfacing and tracing back from that, they picked up a small dinghy being clumsily paddled towards it.

'Bert, you're bang on, but how the hell do we stop her? Give me your rifle, Bert,' said Bonham-Johns. He supported it on a rock, aimed and fired.

'Damn,' he said. He reloaded and aimed again but stopped.

'Bert, what do you think that range is?'

'Probably eight hundred yards and at least two hundred feet below us,' he replied. Bonham-Johns adjusted the sight, took aim again and fired.

'Shit,' he said, 'the dinghy is too far away'. At that moment, flashes of tracer bullets appeared from the conning tower of the U-boat, and within a split second bullets whizzed all around them.

'What the hell?' said Bonham-Johns as they both dived for cover. He pulled himself up and looked over the edge just as bullets ricocheted off the cliff below them, showering rock shards into his face. He rolled back, clutching his head.

'Colonel, are you OK?' Bert yelled.

'I don't know,' said Bonham-Johns, 'I think so, but right now, Bert, it's up to you. You have to stop her.'

'Shoot over the cliffs with the Browning to draw their fire,' said Bert, 'and I'll move along the cliff.'

Bert grabbed the rifle and as Bonham-Johns started to fire the machine gun in short bursts, the U-boat again sprayed the cliff with bullets. Bert ran back from the cliff edge to the safety of the path and ran two hundred feet to a rocky promontory. He knelt down and rested the rifle between two boulders. He took a few seconds to focus and pick up the dinghy. Eight hundred yards, two hundred feet down, light wind from the left, he reminded himself. He took aim and squeezed the trigger. He thought it was a good shot but the dinghy still moved forward. He took aim again, took a deep breath and thought of Clara and Robert and their slashed faces.

'You bastards,' he muttered and tensed every muscle in his body, held his breath, aimed and gently squeezed the trigger. He stared at the target for a few seconds and thought it had stopped. He aimed again and fired. His heart skipped a beat because this time there was definitely something happening; the dinghy was slowly getting smaller; yes, it was sinking.

The U-boat started to fire again, but in the same general direction as before in response to Bonham-Johns's machine gun fire.

Right, you bastards, Bert thought, and aimed at the conning tower. He fired three times using up the last of his bullets.

'I wonder if I got any of the bastards – if only I had a box full of ammo,' he muttered. He looked back, and the U-boat was already slowly disappearing, and in less than thirty seconds it was gone from sight.

Bert ran back to Bonham-Johns.

'The submarine has gone, but importantly without its intended cargo – I got the dinghy.'

'What happened to Bannencourt?' Bonham-Johns asked.

'Well there's no chance of getting out of that freezing water alive, that's for sure. She might be washed up with whatever she had with her in the next few days but most times, folk are never seen again, usually eaten by the conger eels.'

'Bert that's a job well done,' said Bonham-Johns. 'You don't realise how important this is for the country.'

'How are you, sir?' asked Bert, seeing Bonham-Johns's blood-specked face.

'That's the first time you've showed me any respect, sergeant,' he said with a smile. 'I'm fine. You lead the way back to the Telegraph – I have an extremely urgent phone call to make.'

———ᥱᥲ———

Tuesday 6 January 1942 – 6.00 am

Noordwijk, occupied Netherlands

Stefan Merensky looked anxiously at his watch. Klaus Wenger was uncharacteristically late for duty. In his absence, Merensky reviewed the messages that had been placed on Wenger's desk overnight. Towards the top was an intercept of a coded message sent by Kinnenberg in Hvalfjörður to London at 06.10 that morning that read, 'confirm operation harpoon downgraded stop tirpitz in baltic on trials stop washington and wichita rendezvous here 9 jan stop'. He didn't fully appreciate the implications of the message but it was clearly of high priority and he forwarded it to Berlin and Donitz in Lorient.

At 6.35 he looked at his watch again and decided he really had to go and check on Wenger. He looked around the room, and there was an air of concern written on the faces of the whole team. They knew their captain was never late.

'I'll leave you in charge, Werner, I have to go and find the captain. He'll be in serious trouble if he doesn't get here soon.'

Werner Louw was petrified at the prospect of having to explain that Wenger and Merensky were both missing if the colonel came in.

Merensky ran to the Abwehr billet but the door to Wenger's room was locked and he had to get one of the staff to open it. He was not there and, more to the point, his bed had not been slept in. He knew he should report this immediately, but how could he report his boss was missing and get him into serious trouble?

Merensky knew Wenger had been going to meet his Dutch girlfriend, Caja, last night at De Oude Molen and that she had arranged a room for them nearby. Did he spend the night with her? He wondered if he should go to the inn and try and find out where they'd gone, but that was fifteen minutes away plus another fifteen minutes to find the room, and he'd be gone from his post for at least an hour. That was a court-martial offence.

After a further minute's indecision, he ran back to the operations room. The whole team watched him walk in and sit at his desk. Werner Louw looked as though he was saying a prayer of thanks.

Merensky, still short of breath, picked up the phone and dialled the colonel in charge of the Abwehr. The whole team looked at him with consternation and he hesitated momentarily.

'Can I speak with Colonel Rosenkranz, please? It's Special Operator Stefan Merensky.'

When he put the phone down, his face was pale and he was sweating.

Two minutes later the door to the operations room opened and Colonel Rosenkranz marched in. He was well-liked by the team but was a stickler for discipline and looked distinctly agitated. The entire team stood to attention and saluted.

'At ease,' snapped Rosenkranz. 'Now, tell me, Merensky, what the hell is going on here?'

'Sir, the captain must be sick or injured because he hasn't reported for duty today,' blurted Merensky.

'Have you spoken with him?'

'No, sir, I haven't.'

'So how the hell do you know he's sick?' Merensky's silence provided the answer.

'Have you looked for him?'

'Yes, sir, his room has not been slept in.'

Rosenkranz took his cap off and scratched his bald head. He looked undecided. He glanced at his watch.

'I have orders to report missing officers, I've got no alternative but to communicate this immediately.'

'But sir, I'm sure he'll be here shortly,' Merensky blurted out. Rosenkranz looked at him and just shook his head and walked out.

Ten minutes later, the door to the operations room opened and Colonel Rosenkranz walked in followed by two Gestapo officers. Merensky hadn't expected that – no one had. The atmosphere in the room went ice-cold, and the mood changed from consternation to outright fear. The situation had escalated out of control, and Merensky wondered if he'd done the right thing.

The senior Gestapo officer, Oberst Rossing, introduced himself.

'Who is Merensky?' he snapped.

Merensky put his hand up.

'You, come with me, and everyone else stop what you are doing and remain silent until I tell you differently.'

He led Merensky out of the door and Rosenkranz followed. One Gestapo officer remained in the decoding room, and the team knew there was serious trouble. They exchanged fearful glances but said nothing. A wet stain appeared on Werner Louw's trousers.

In an adjoining office, Rossing sat behind the desk, not offering Rosenkranz or Merensky a seat.

'Right, Merensky, why did you not report that Captain Wenger had failed to turn up for duty this morning?' demanded Rossing, glaring at him.

'Sir, I have never, ever known the captain report late before. He is a stickler for punctuality. I thought he must be sick.' He hesitated but knew he had to tell the truth; there would have been witnesses.

'After about thirty minutes I quickly went to his room in the billet to check on him, but he was not there and his bed had not been slept in, so I came straight back to phone the colonel, sir.' He felt it sounded a pretty weak explanation.

'Merensky, we were informed at 7.20 am, and Wenger was supposed to be on duty at 6.00 am,' said Rossing. 'You know the rules on reporting, as do you, colonel.'

Merensky stared straight ahead and said nothing. He knew he was in deep trouble. Rosenkranz looked uneasy at his sudden implication.

'Who was the captain meeting last night?'

'As far as I know, he was meeting his girlfriend for a drink at De Oude Molen. He left here at around 8.30 pm and said he'd be in bright and early this morning.'

'Who is this girl?'

'Her name is Caja. She's Dutch ... he's known her for a couple of weeks as far as I am aware.'

'Surname, address?'

Merensky thought for a moment and shook his head.

'Sorry, sir, I don't know. I don't remember him ever mentioning her surname, and I've never met her.'

'No matter. It'll be a bogus name anyway,' said the Gestapo officer dismissively. 'Captain Wenger is not the first German officer to go missing in recent weeks. A captain in the Marine-Flak Abteilung was missing for nearly a week and found floating in the canal off of Bornstraat yesterday. He had been bludgeoned and strangled,' said the Gestapo officer. 'He was assassinated. Two days later a Leutnant with the Engineering Group went missing, and today, Captain Wenger. The one common thread in the three cases is De Oude Molen – they had all been drinking in there the night they disappeared.'

Merensky wanted to point out that dozens of German soldiers and officers drank there every night, but he kept that thought to himself.

'Colonel, no one leaves this building until I return,' said Rossing, and with that he marched out.

Rosenkranz visibly relaxed with the Gestapo officer's departure.

'Merensky, they suspect it's a Dutch Resistance attack. They think the girl was a honey trap.'

'Jesus Christ, sir, several of the team have Dutch girlfriends.'

'Well we'll have to let them know and tell them to tread carefully. Let's go and speak with them,' said Rosenkranz.

When they left his office the second Gestapo Officer was now pacing the front entrance. Rosenkranz and Merensky entered the operations room and everyone stared at them expectantly. Rosenkranz addressed them.

'As you know, Captain Wenger has not reported for duty this morning and the Gestapo are trying to find him. He was due to meet a girl called Caja at the De Oude Molen last night. Did anyone see him at the Inn and does anyone know who this Caja is?' He looked at a sea of blank faces.

Before he'd had chance to tell them about the apparent 'honey trap', the door opened and the Gestapo Officer who had been guarding the entrance marched in.

Rosenkranz glared at him and said, 'A moment of your time, please, outside.' Closing the door behind him he went on. 'I want to question my staff about last night, ask who knows this Caja and if anybody has seen her. Information will not be forthcoming with you there unless, of course, you intend to interrogate each and every one of them at Gestapo Head Quarters. Do I need to remind you the information we handle here is top secret and every team member has the highest security clearance? If anyone knows anything, I will inform you. We must find out as much as we can and get back to work. Every minute we're not working means that crucial strategic information is being missed.'

The Gestapo officer looked at him disapprovingly.

'Colonel Rosenkranz, you heard Oberst Rossing's orders, "stop what you are doing and remain silent until I tell you otherwise". What don't you understand about such a simple instruction?'

Rosenkranz shook his head at the sheer stupidity of it and returned to the operations room. Everyone sat in silence and contemplated serious trouble.

Fifteen minutes later, Oberst Rossing returned followed by two SS soldiers.

'Arrest this man for deserting his post. Take him away,' he barked, pointing at Merensky. Rosenkranz was incensed.

'You have no grounds to arrest my senior operator. He has nothing to do with Captain Wenger's disappearance. Release him at once.'

'Colonel, I am placing you under arrest also, for failing to report a missing senior officer,' said Rossing. 'I trust you will not be any trouble. Come with me.'

As they left, the remaining Abwehr team were in shock and in disbelief. The remaining Gestapo officer sat in Wenger's chair and glared at them. Werner Louw had his head in his hands and was visibly shaking.

The messages that had been monitored and recorded between 6.30 am and 7.30 am remained largely unchecked on Wenger's desk. The messages being transmitted by the Allies after that time went unrecorded and unchecked. At 8 am they missed a coded message sent by Thornton: 'for daggoo stop confirm harpoon active stop proceed sullom voe stop eta 8th stop'.

Tuesday 6 January 1942 – 10.00 pm

Cabinet War Rooms, London

Bonham-Johns arrived at the Cabinet War Rooms with two senior members of MI5. They entered the outer office.

'We have an appointment with Mr Churchill please, Sir Alistair,' said Bonham-Johns.

'Let me see if he's available,' said Sir Alistair as he picked up the phone.

'Show them in,' said the voice. Sir Alistair ushered them into the small, smoky office.

'Ah, Julian,' said Churchill, 'oh my boy you do look a bit of a mess. What happened?'

'Sir, I got on the wrong end of a U-boat cannon,' said Bonham-Johns. 'I believe you know Brigadier Clifford Latcham and Major Courtney Mills.'

'I do indeed,' said Churchill, shaking their hands.

'Right, gentlemen, we have an internal problem to clear up I believe: a not insignificant matter of one of our staff working for the Germans,' said Churchill.

'Sir, before we start, I regret that I need to tender my resignation as your Personal Operations Liaison Officer,' said Bonham-Johns hesitantly. 'It's in the matter of my fraternising with the member of staff you mentioned.' Churchill stared at him with a hint of a smile.

'Mmm, an indiscretion it certainly appears, Julian. Very regrettable. Courtney, your team has investigated this and I want your findings. Better fill us in on matters, please.'

'Mr Churchill, we have been questioning Lucy McCloud overnight, and she has provided a lot of crucial information on the spy network we have been tracking. This particular plot takes us back to South Africa where there is strong support for the Germans within the ranks of the Afrikaners and from over the border in what was German South West Africa. They have a common dislike for the British as a result of both losing their homeland and the Boer War. Indeed, Mr Churchill, you were captured by the Boers in 1899 so have first-hand experience of how high these feelings run.'

Churchill nodded but said nothing.

Courtney went on. 'One of the rotten apples was a certain Godfried Bannencourt. He fought for Germany in WW1 and sailed back to South West Africa in 1920, only to find that the territory was under the control of Britain, and had been made a South African League of Nations protectorate. Through his contacts, he joined the resistance to get his homeland back under the control of the German colonials. He was a marine biologist by training and was able to get a job just across the border in Alexander Bay on the Cape West Coast in the newly formed Department of Fisheries. He became a well-respected authority on the Southern Right Whale – it was a perfect cover for his activities. He was able to provide support by receiving smuggled diamonds from South West Africa, selling them on the black market and returning arms and money back to them.'

He married Eleanor Davie in 1925 and when the authorities became suspicious of his movements to and from Alexander Bay, he and his wife escaped to De Aar in the middle of the Karoo desert. It's a major railway junction and about as remote as you can get. However, he was betrayed by one of his contacts, and he was found and assassinated in 1934.'

'Shortly after, Eleanor left South Africa and came to the UK, but she remained bitter and twisted at the involvement of the South African Government in her husband's death. She disappeared and we didn't know where she was – until now. Eleanor's older sister, Maureen Davie, married Carel McCloud and they had a daughter, Lucy. Now, because of a botch-up by the security forces, Maureen and Carel were killed in the same explosion as Godfried but there was one other who also died: Rodmond Lauterbach. He was also a German South West Africa sympathiser and had a son, Roden Lauterbach, who came to Britain five years ago and changed his name to Rodney Lavine. He's the enemy agent at Porthcurno, otherwise known as Agent Stiletto. Now, Julian, you'll be wondering where Lucy McCloud fits in?' added Mills.

'I think I can guess,' said Bonham-Johns, rubbing his face.

'Well maybe, maybe not,' said Mills.

'When the Nazis recruited Eleanor Bannencourt in 1939 they also recruited Lucy McCloud. Her parents had after all been killed by the pro-British security services in Pretoria. Although they weren't close, her Aunt Eleanor put her London contact onto Lucy. So when Lucy applied for the job here, we thoroughly researched her background as we do for everyone and established her link with German sympathisers.

'We put her in front of "The Twenty Committee" – that's named after the Roman numerals "XX" for double cross – and, long story short, she agreed to become a double agent. We fed her information, often out-of-date, often ambiguous, and I'm sorry to say, Julian, allowed her to develop a relationship with you to add credibility for her Nazi handlers.'

Bonham-Johns stared at Mills, open-mouthed.

'You did what?' he said. 'You encouraged a double agent to come on to me? That's bloody despicable,' said Bonham-Johns, exasperated. 'How can you sit there and tell me that to my face?'

There was a long silence.

'It wasn't like that, Julian, you have my word. There was no instruction, no coercion, no pressure. I believe what Lucy did was entirely spontaneous.'

'And you did nothing about it because it was beneficial to the bluff?' added Bonham-Johns, shaking his head at the irony of it all. 'Look, if Lucy McCloud was part of this agent cell she must have known the location of Eleanor Bannencourt and the details of the plot,' said Bonham-Johns.

'Well, Julian, you might think that, but you see, Lucy is not Agent Violin!' Bonham-Johns stared at Mills in astonishment. Again, there was a long silence and even Churchill was captivated by the intrigue; his cigar had gone out.

'Eleanor Bannencourt is, or rather was, Agent Banjo. Agent Violin, we have now found out, is none other than Rodney Lavine's mistress, Valerie.

Bonham-Johns shook his head, trying to take it all in.

'But the telephone number on the piece of paper that Lavine had in his pocket is the same one that Lucy gave me. Why?'

'Yes that's right. It's a shared line at 6 Pitts Head Street in Mayfair. Valerie, Agent Violin, lives on the fourth floor and Lucy on the first floor but they did not communicate directly. Lucy was unaware of Valerie and communicated to the person she thought was Agent Violin, who was in fact an intermediary. My MI5 agent lives on the second floor to watch Lucy, and you can only imagine our surprise when we discovered Agent Violin was living on the fourth floor.

Churchill smiled and chuckled silently to himself, and relit the cigar that had received no attention since the discussion had started. It was clear to everyone the amazing web of intrigue and espionage that had gone into the exercise. Mills was enjoying himself.

'So what happens now?' asked Bonham-Johns.

'Well, we don't believe Lucy has been working as a triple agent – that is, pretending to be a double agent for the Allies, whilst she is actually a double agent for the Germans. There's absolutely no evidence of that. She's currently at a safe house and she will continue to act as a double agent for the duration of the war, or until we decide otherwise. She's still useful to us. Her cover hasn't been blown to the best of our knowledge.'

'Violin, on the other hand, is not being cooperative, as you can imagine, particularly in light of what happened to Lavine. We'll continue to work her. It's amazing what the threat of a firing squad can do to change people's minds. I have one of my female operatives covering for her at the moment, and we'll keep that going as long as we can. The intermediary is in prison and singing like a canary.'

There was a long silence.

'So, Julian, I will not accept your resignation,' said Churchill. 'Remember I said to you that in wartime the truth is so precious that she should always be attended by a bodyguard of lies? Well, this is a case in point, my boy. Collectively we're greater than the sum of us as individuals. So it's business as usual, gentlemen. Now, it appears we are back in damage-limitation mode over the Porthcurno Telegraph Station. Julian, fill us in on what happened and the next steps in Operation Harpoon.'

Wednesday 7 January 1942 – 5.00 pm

Westerland Island, Germany

Based on intelligence received by the Abwehr listening station at Noordwijk Admiral Raeder had delayed the planned sailing of Tirpitz to Trondheim by 24 hours. However, as part of the subterfuge, she had slipped her moorings at Princes Dock, Wilhelmshaven, at 11 pm the previous night and had sailed north one hundred nautical miles and set anchor off the west coast of Denmark in the lee of the of island of Westerland. Captain Karl Topp had been very pleased with the performance of both ship and crew. As the weather forecast had predicted, it had been wet and squally all day with low cloud, and he was confident they had not been spotted by sea or air.

British military intelligence had decrypted the Enigma messages sent by the German navy and had detected the departure of the vessel, but the weather had not allowed any aerial reconnaissance.

Through the evening the weather had improved, and the crew was on high alert, scanning the sky for enemy aircraft. The sirens had started wailing minutes before when a watchful but anxious sailor had thought he'd heard aircraft. The lookouts fore and aft and on the bridge searched the sky as the search lights criss-crossed. The cloud layer was at 5,000 feet, so an Allied spotter plane should have been visible, if it was there in the first place.

Tirpitz was due to weigh anchor with her three escorts at 6 pm, but, back in Pontchâteau, Raeder was still in a quandary as to where to send her. The message they had sent before destroying the Porthcurno Telegraph had definitely been received and had been confirmed by Thornton in Hvalfjörður, but the sailing was recorded as one day later than the agreed message. This was compounded by a 12-hour security shut down of the Noordwijk facility. As a consequence, there was no new intelligence on USS Tuscaloosa. Radio traffic indicated that Washington and Wichita had left Scapa Flow yesterday, sailing north, but the bad weather had precluded any U-boat confirmation of this. Raeder had a dilemma on what to do with his prize battleship.

At 5.50 pm Captain Topp received his orders: 'Proceed to Trondheim at full speed.'

The twelve Wagner superheated boilers were fired to maximum and precisely on the hour she weighed anchor and started for her first Arctic adventure.

Wednesday 8 April 1942 – 4.00 pm

Thames Embankment, London

Hindsight is a wonderful thing, thought Bonham-Johns as he reflected on the twists and turns of the last three months. He was sitting on a bench overlooking the Thames and its busy docks with ships from around the World disgorging their cargo to an insatiable, war-torn Britain.

There was some good news: Losses associated with the Arctic Convoys had reduced; in part because of the Navy heavyweights from the USA but also due to the excellent organisation and coordination out of Hvalfjörður. In the Mediterranean, Malta had been held but with a huge loss of men and ships, and the Italian 10th Army had been pushed back five hundred miles in North Africa, opening up the potential for an attack on a weakened and demoralised Italy.

But there was no good news on Tirpitz; she was still elusive. 617 Squadron had destroyed the Beitstadfjord fuel depot with heavy loss of aircraft and air crew, and the RAF was poised to obliterate Fættenfjord when she and her escorts docked; but the prize never showed up and the operation was cancelled.

USS Washington and USS Wichita had sailed towards Iceland ready to back-track at a moment's notice, and USS Tuscaloosa hid in the Shetlands awaiting the giant battleship's appearance, which never came. Whilst on patrol, Tuscaloosa was spotted and attacked by U-101 that was, ironically, heading from the Arctic Ocean to support Tirpitz sailing north. Looking back that was probably the turning point.

When Tirpitz sailed from the island of Westerland with her three escorts, she moved north as expected and was two hundred miles southwest of Stavanger in Norway when U-101 sent a message confirming she'd engaged the Tuscaloosa south of the Shetlands. Admiral Raeder smelled a rat. Tirpitz was ordered to turn due-east into the Skagerrak, around the north of Denmark, and then south through the Kattegat, passing within sight of

Copenhagen and on into the Baltic Sea, just as Thornton had suggested she might.

Bonham-Johns chuckled to himself and shook his head. You could put whatever spin you wished on the Nazis' decision, but it seemed clear that the Third Reich was not prepared to risk an untested battleship with a new crew against some of the Allies' mightiest warships. The Allies had come so close to setting the perfect trap, but the battle for Tirpitz was still to come.

Churchill had said, 'We know where she is, we will patiently watch her every move, we will scheme and we will plan and eventually she will be ours.' He certainly had a way with words, thought Bonham-Johns.

Bonham-Johns was looking forward to a visit to West Cornwall later that week. Bert Chenoweth and Robert Chenoweth had both been awarded the George Medal for exceptional bravery and Will Tarraway the Military Medal, and he had been asked by Churchill to present them in person. Harry Nancarrow was awarded the King's Commendation for Brave Conduct. Poacher turned war hero, he thought, again chuckling at the implausibility. He could only imagine the barracking Harry would get for it but, credit where credit's due, not many civilians can say they've killed a German special forces soldier with a Cornish shovel.

He was not looking forward to the other task during the visit. There was to be a memorial service in St Levan church for those who had been killed in the attack on Security Area 28. He was to lay wreaths on behalf of the King and the Prime Minister. Porthcurno and the surrounding hamlets were scarred by the terror and death visited on their remote community. Three civilians, twelve British soldiers, five German soldiers and two enemy agents had died; and for what?

'Absolutely bloody nothing,' Bonham-Johns muttered.

He still thought of Lucy every day. He knew he was in love with her, despite all that had happened. The touch of her hand, the warmth of her smile and the twinkle of her eye contact made him ache for her. He wanted her so much.

After two months, he had plucked up the courage to write to

her and gave the letter to Major Mills to deliver. He had received a short reply back and he'd memorised and treasured every word:

My darling Julian,
I too love you with all my heart and wish things between us were different. I think of you all the time and you are the only light in my dull life. But my deceit and exploitation of you hurts me so much I cannot bear it. It casts an impenetrable shadow on my life. I hope and pray that with the passing of time this darkness will lift.
With all my love, always,
Lucy

Bonham-Johns sat staring at the river, his vision blurring as tears welled up and trickled down his cheeks, as they had done so many times in the past weeks. Yes hindsight is a wonderful thing, he thought, as the air raid sirens sounded, yet again, across the East End of London.